D0467376

AND OTHER THINGS TO

TOSS

IN A

BLENDER

Lisa Greenwald

Random House New York

This is a work of fiction. Names, characters, places, and incidents either are the product of the author's imagination or are used fictitiously. Any resemblance to actual persons, living or dead, events, or locales is entirely coincidental.

 Published in the United States by Random House Children's Books, a division of Penguin Random House LLC, New York.

Random House and the colophon are registered trademarks of Penguin Random House LLC.

Visit us on the Web! randomhouseteens.com

Educators and librarians, for a variety of teaching tools, visit us at RHTeachersLibrarians.com

Library of Congress Cataloging-in-Publication Data is available upon request.

ISBN 978-0-399-55638-8 (trade) — ISBN 978-0-399-55640-1 (ebook)

Printed in the United States of America
10 9 8 7 6 5 4 3 2 1
First Edition

Random House Children's Books supports the First Amendment and celebrates the right to read.

FOR JODIE, PARTNER IN CRIME

CONTENTS

LIVIN' THE DREAM

Coconut, peaches, banana,
raspberries, vanilla frozen yogurt

MIA

Justine's full-length mirror was magical. We weren't sure if it was the way it hung on the wall, or the specific tint of the glass. Sometimes we thought the floor in her room was uneven and that was what caused it. It's not like we spent forever trying to figure out why we looked great in it; we were just grateful that we did.

"Okay, go sit," she instructed. "Because people always check themselves out in a full-length so they know how an outfit works standing up. But you may spend a lot of time sitting at this party. I don't know. We need to get all perspectives."

"Right." I moved over to her desk chair. "Like this?"

"Sit more on the edge," she insisted. "People always sit on the edge of chairs at parties."

"They do?" I squinted and readjusted myself.

She stood back with a finger on her lip. "Perfect. You look so good in navy. Also, terry is so sensible because, I don't know, you may need to use it to dry off. Will Adia really have towels for all of us?" She paused and I wasn't sure if she was asking me or just thinking out loud. She walked over and tousled my hair. "I think you have your summer-blond highlights already, and it's only June. Go you."

"Yeah?" I stood up and went back to the mirror to check out my hair.

"Definitely." She put an arm around me, and we admired ourselves. "We're hot, what can I say?"

I laughed. "Yeah, right."

"Okay, my turn," Justine said, walking over to her closet.

I kicked off my flip-flops and leaned back on her bed. I turned up the playlist—a mix of current favorites and old classics—we'd made for the end of school.

"Hey, where did we go?" Justine sang with her back to me as she wriggled into the lacey white cover-up. *"Days when the rains came?"*

She slipped her feet into her black platform flip-flops and turned around. "So?"

"Love. One hundred percent love," I said.

"Come on." She glared, pulling her brown curls back into a low ponytail. "Really? You can't mean that."

"I can," I defended myself. "I love it. Your legs look super toned and, like, tan already, and the cover-up is subtle enough to be a cute sundress. But also not like over-the-top *look at me, I'm in a dress*. Ya know?"

"Promise?" She stared at herself in the mirror.

I walked over to her. "Promise."

"Was the bathing suit okay?" she asked, grabbing a lip color from her vanity table and testing it out. I followed her over there to do the same. "I mean, it's just plain black. So whatevs. But it's not mom-ish, right?"

"Definitely not mom-ish." I pursed my lips, trying on a lip gloss. "How's this color?"

"Go a little redder." She handed me another tube. "This one'll be good."

I tried it, and she nodded in approval.

"Can we go?" I asked. "The longer we wait, the more nervous I get."

"Well, it's still really early, and we definitely can't be the first ones there." She plopped down on her window seat. "We'll leave in ten minutes and drive around first."

I pulled my hair away from my neck and rubbed the sweat off with my hand. I had a gravelly, rumbly feeling in my stomach. I paced back and forth, trying to calm down. I wondered if Seth and I would sneak away from the party to hook up in the pool shed or something. Maybe he'd say *Let's go for a walk* and we'd find some secluded spot only he knew about.

"I know I've asked you this a hundred times, but do you honestly think Julian and I are gonna hook up tonight?" Justine asked. "Do you know for sure he's into me?"

"I don't know for sure, but I mentioned it to Seth and he thought it was a good idea. . . ." I motioned for her to move over on the window seat so I could sit down. "I feel like you'd be cute together."

"We would be, right?" She smiled, pulling her knees up to her chin. "Julian and Justine. It sounds good. We could *both* have boyfriends this summer, Mia. How insane would that be?"

"Pretty insane," I said, scrolling through Instagram. I loved the inspiring quote accounts.

Go confidently in the direction of your dreams.
Live the life you have always imagined.
HENRY DAVID THOREAU

"Do you think I'm living the life I've always imagined?" I asked Justine. "I am, right?"

She rolled her eyes and gently kicked my knee. "Oh, man. You and your quotes."

I shrugged. "Can we please go? I can't sit here anymore!"

"Fine," she said. "When we're in the car, please coach me on how to talk to Julian. How to be flirty, but not too flirty. Give me interesting topics to discuss. Maybe an inspirational quote or two. Okay?"

"Okay." I checked myself out in the mirror one last time.

Justine said, "Oh, wait—one more thing." She grabbed the bottle of cherry blossom body splash off her dresser and spritzed the air. "Walk into it. Walk into it."

I sniffed. "I feel like I smell like a cherry Jolly Rancher."

"Now we're ready," she replied. "We are so ready."

And I believed her. I always believed her.

MELONCHOLY

Melon, blackberries, soy milk, Swiss chard

MIA

Justine and I were in a heated game of Virgin/Nonvirgin, pretty much our favorite game.

"Oh, text from Alexis," I said when we heard both of our phones chime at the same time.

Alexis: Having fun, girlies?

Mia: Yup, miss you!

Justine: Samey. We'll give you a full report after the party.

Alexis: Promise?

Justine: Duh

Mia: xoxo

"She is so pissed she's missing this," Justine said, putting her phone in her bag. "I don't get why she has to be at her dad's for, like, the whole summer. I mean, school just ended."

"I know. I feel bad." I kept looking for Seth out of the corner of my eye. Like, I was looking for him, but I didn't want anyone to notice that I was looking for him. I could feel his presence, though. Every part of me was on high alert.

Seth. My boyfriend. We were at a pool party together.

It didn't even seem real.

I was never the girl with the boyfriend. I never even *thought* I'd be the girl with the boyfriend.

I sat facing Justine on the lounge chair, trying to act like I was really involved in the game and not obsessing about Seth.

"Okay, Abby Sanders. Go," Justine said after a sip of punch.

"Oh, definitely non," I declared like it was a well-known fact. "Owen Umberg. Winter break. Remember? The whole thing about the back of his mom's Pathfinder."

Justine nodded. "Right. Duh." She looked around, searching for another victim. "Craig Aronson."

"Virgin. I think." I tilted my head, unsure. "Right? Unless there was more to the Craig-and-Samantha two-week relationship of sophomore year."

"Yeah, I'd say virgin." She drank the rest of her punch in one quick gulp. "You think anyone plays this using us?"

I shook my head. "Doubt it. I don't think anyone even thinks of us, or notices us . . . and if they do, they know we're virgins."

She pondered that for a second. "Yeah, I guess you're right. But I bet people totally think you're doing it with Manzell."

"Really?" I squealed. I wasn't having sex, but the notion that people *thought* I was having sex—that felt good.

I stroked my smooth after-haircut hair.

Everything felt perfect.

Justine left the lounge chairs to go to the bathroom, scope out the scene, and get us more punch. She was driving that night, so she was drinking the nonalcoholic kind. But she pretended it was alcoholic. Justine was good at tricking her mind.

All around me boys were throwing girls over their shoulders like it was nothing. Like the girls were silky laundry bags holding only a few pairs of underwear.

These were the skinny girls in the little bikinis. Their stomachs stayed flat without them even having to try.

The Adia Montgomerys of the world. The Laurel Pecks.

I wondered what it was like to be one of those girls. Did life literally seem amazing every single second of the day? How did the air feel against their bare stomachs? What was it like to never have to suck in—to never have to sit with a pillow over your middle at a slumber party?

I'd never be one of those girls. Not even if I starved myself for the rest of my life.

But that was okay. We couldn't *all* be the skinny girl. The world needed the slightly chubby girls to balance things out.

I looked around for Seth, debating if I should go and find him. But I didn't want anyone to take these lounge chairs. I had to wait until Justine got back.

A few minutes later, I spotted him, walking out from behind the grill with Adia.

Julian Glazer was flipping hamburgers in the air and serving hot dogs on skewers. I guessed Adia had made him grillmaster, or maybe he'd begged for the job.

It was odd that Seth hadn't tried to find me right away, and it was odder that he and Adia were hanging out. But none of it was *that* odd. I was paranoid, always feeling like bad news was lurking around the corner.

I watched Seth coming over to me, and I quickly looked away like I wasn't watching him even though I totally was. My heart felt slippery.

"Hey." He sat down on the edge of the lounge chair and scratched his cheek. There were people all around us, but no one was really paying attention. I wanted to pull him close and start kissing him right there.

"Hey." I smiled, putting my feet up on his legs. My pinky-peach pedicure was fresh and perfect.

"Mia, we have to talk," he said, shifting away from me a little bit. "I just don't know, like, about us."

"Um," I started to reply, looking around. I couldn't tell if other people were hearing this or not. I sat back against the lounge chair and took my feet off him. "What do you mean?"

He rubbed his Birkenstock back and forth on the poolside pavement. "I just don't think I can do this."

"Do what?" I asked him.

It was hard to hear what he was saying with all the noise around us. Pool water splashed against the pavement and music blasted from the outdoor speakers. Girls clumped together, laughing, like everything in the world was hilarious. Guys screamed at each other to *check this out.*

We'd been looking forward to this party for weeks. There was even talk of skinny-dipping, though I hadn't fully committed to it yet. I wasn't really a candidate for skinny-dipping. But maybe if it was dark? Really, really dark would be okay.

"I just can't be in a relationship right now. . . ."

I stared at Seth as he talked, but I couldn't make eye contact. I focused on his neck. I loved that neck. And then I noticed something. It looked like Seth had a hickey. But that was impossible. Hickeys weren't a thing. I definitely hadn't given him a hickey. Sunburn, maybe? Some kind of allergic reaction?

I wondered if anyone had an EpiPen.

"Mia, I'm so sorry," he said finally, and in that moment I guess he really did look sorry. Whatever sorry looks like. A combination of wimpy and tired, I guess. He took his hat off and twisted a little curl on the top of his head around and around and around. "I just need to be on my own right now." He looked me right in the eyes, and then down at the pavement.

I scoffed, "On your own? It's summer. You have nothing going on."

I don't know why I debated it or even continued the conversation. I knew it only made me look more pathetic.

I kept staring at the blotch on his neck. It seemed like it might be growing. What exactly had happened behind the grill with Adia? I was too scared to want to know.

I covered my stomach with my arms.

Get out. Get out now, I pleaded with myself.

"I'm sorry," he said again, putting his hat back on. "I'll see ya around, though."

He stood up and swaggered away, the butt of his cargo shorts drooping more and more with each step he took.

I used to love his walk. I always thought it showed confidence. But now I hated it. Now I wanted to punch that swagger in the face.

I tried to get up, but I was frozen on that lounge, staring out into the party abyss.

"I think Manzell and Mia just broke up," I overheard someone say, but I didn't have the energy to look over and see who it was.

"Like, right now?" another kid replied.

I scanned the crowd for Justine, but I couldn't see her. I stayed there, sitting up, looking out into the crowd, at nothing in particular, like I was waiting for something to happen. My mind was blank; I had no idea what to do.

"What's going on?" Justine asked when she came back, two sweating cups of fruit punch in her hands.

"We broke up," I told her.

"What?" She recoiled.

"Isn't it weird how we say *we broke up,* but really it wasn't a *we* thing at all? It was completely a *him* thing. All him. He broke up with me."

"No. That is not okay." Justine dropped the cups and made no attempt to pick them up. Fruit punch spilled all over the grass. She wasn't the type of girl to drop things and not pick them up. Her mom was really into manners and stuff. Right and wrong. A firm believer in thank-you notes.

Justine grabbed my hand. "We need to get out of here. Come on."

We got into Justine's car, and she sped through the winding Bridgefield streets. We weren't in a rush to get anywhere, though. In fact, staying in her old Buick seemed to be the most pleasant plan.

When you're going somewhere, things are never as painful. You're literally moving so it's pretty much impossible to feel stuck. It's like you never really want to get where you're going. You just want to stay in the car, on the journey.

You want to feel like you're on the way to better times.

COMFORT–ME COCONUT

Coconut water, apples, spinach, bananas

JUSTINE

"Cheese fries?" I asked Mia, even though it wasn't really a question. "You need cheese fries."

I clutched the steering wheel, trying to drive safely in the darkness.

I wasn't sure if I should tell Mia what I'd seen, or not. Would knowing make it better or worse?

People say *the truth will set you free,* but I'm not even sure that's true. They also say *ignorance is bliss*. It can't be both, so which is it?

"Okay, yeah," Mia mumbled, staring straight ahead. "Cheese fries."

I had to help her, but I had no idea how. What do you do when your best friend's first boyfriend breaks up with her? What do you say? Especially when you've never had a boyfriend yourself.

My heart felt like it was cracking, like a thin patch of ice on the sidewalk. "It's gonna be okay, Mi," I said.

She shook her head slowly, like she knew that wasn't true.

It was quiet in the car after that. I knew she didn't want to talk. When you've been best friends for as long as we have, you can just tell these things.

I met Mia on the first day of kindergarten. We were assigned to the same table—the green one. Each table in Ms. T's kindergarten class was a different color.

We had to draw self-portraits with a loved one, and she chose her dad.

"I don't have a mom anymore," she said as we colored. "She died a long time ago."

I remember my throat stinging when she said it. After that I always picked her first when we played Seven-Up. When she asked to share my snack, I said yes every time, even if I didn't want to.

She didn't have a mom. She deserved everything else.

"Did you only become my friend because you felt bad for me?" Mia squawked from her sleeping bag during one of our late-night sleepover conversations. We were in seventh grade then, and it seemed like we had so many things to figure out.

"No," I answered to the darkness. "I mean, maybe a little. I was only five. But it doesn't really matter how or why we became friends. What matters is that we *stayed* friends."

"I guess," she replied. "Yeah, you're probably right."

I remember that sleepover specifically because we were so

proud of ourselves that we stayed up past two in the morning, just talking.

I turned into the diner parking lot and looked over at Mia again. She was staring out the window, chewing on the edge of her thumbnail.

We walked into the diner, and Gus, the manager, greeted us. "Ladies." He dipped his head. "Welcome back."

"Thanks, Gus." I smiled and wondered if he could sense that we weren't our usual selves. Mia stared into space, not focusing on anything in particular.

"No Alexis tonight?"

"Nah, she's away for the summer," I answered.

Gus nodded, and we followed him to our favorite booth in the back, by the window. Mia slumped in across the vinyl seat and looked at her phone.

"What's going on?" I asked. "Did he text you?"

"No. I wish," she said softly, and then rested her phone on the table. "I don't even understand what happened."

"Me neither." I shook my head. "Is it weird that we're at the diner in our bathing suits and cover-ups?"

She laughed for a second. "Guess we didn't need to spend so long figuring out these outfits."

I looked up at the waitress who had come to take our order; she wasn't one of the regulars. "We'll have two coffees and an order of cheese fries. Mozzarella. Thank you."

Mia put her head down on the table, and it was gross, but obviously not our biggest problem. "But I still love him," she said. "It's not fair."

"Mia, pick your head up," I whispered. "People are looking at us."

"I don't care," she said, but then she sat up. Her hair was in her face, and she pushed it away. "Remember that night when Seth first talked to me? After the band concert?"

I nodded as the waitress brought over our coffees.

"And I totally thought he was just being friendly, how he brought up my Inca village from fourth grade," she continued. "He honestly remembered my whole project!"

"Yeah, he has a good memory," I said, my heart collapsing. "Definitely."

"And did I tell you he said he'd liked me for a while, before we even talked?" She leaned forward. "Since we helped with freshman orientation in September!"

"Yeah, you mentioned that," I said softly.

I had to tell her the truth. Maybe after the cheese fries. Then I'd tell her.

"I just don't get it." She sniffled. "I mean, what changed? What did I do wrong?"

"Nothing!" I yelled, louder than I'd intended. "You didn't do anything wrong! Boys are dumb, and people change their minds sometimes. And it's stupid. And unfair."

She sipped her coffee, and then the cheese fries came.

"I can't eat this," she said. "My stomach hurts."

She'd come around. She couldn't just let a beautiful plate of cheese fries sit in front of her and not eat them. I pulled a fry out and lost some of the mozzarella on the table.

"And remember when he helped my dad with our Wi-Fi?" she asked. "He's so clueless with that stuff, but Seth didn't even mind helping him."

"I know," I said, burning my mouth on a cheese fry. "That was nice."

I figured this was what best friends were supposed to do. Listen to all the memories, one after another, and be supportive. If I kept doing it, eventually she'd feel better. Maybe not today. Or tomorrow. But it wouldn't be like this forever.

"I thought we were going to be together all summer, and then senior year, and go to prom, and I worried what we would do about long distance when we went to college, but I figured we'd work it out," Mia went on and on. "I mean, he wants to go to Brown and I'm gonna apply early to Amherst so it's not that far and . . ." She slumped forward onto the table again, crying.

I picked one of her golden-brown hairs out of the cheese fries and threw it on the floor. "Mi, I know, it sucks so much," I said.

"Why even bother liking someone?" She threw her head back. "There's no point! I'd be better off if I never went out with him!"

Okay, so I wasn't going to tell her now. . . .

Maybe I'd never tell her. Maybe that's what best friends do—they protect. But other people had seen what happened, so it was only a matter of time before she'd find out on her own, and then she'd be mad I didn't tell her.

"No, I mean, he gave you that awesome clarinet cell phone case," I said, half-shrugging. "That was worth it. You'll always have band class!"

"Justine!" she snapped, ripping off the case, trying to cut it in pieces with the diner knife. "I know you're trying to lighten the mood, but stop."

"You left your heart all vulnerable, and now you're leaving your phone the same way."

Mia rolled her eyes, but then she laughed, and finally took a cheese fry.

"And remember that night when you, me, and Alexis went over to his house to study for the history midterm?" she started again. "And he made guacamole! And it was really good. Like as good as Dos Caminos?"

"I remember," I said. "It was good. He was generous with the lime."

Mia gulped the rest of her coffee. "And once he quizzed me on science and he kissed me every time I got a question right."

I swallowed hard and picked at the cheese fries. I let her go on and on and on.

FIND YOUR POWER

Protein powder, peaches, kale, banana, peanut butter

MIA

We were back in the car, on the way to Justine's house from the diner, and every few minutes, I'd forget that anything had even happened. I'd go to text Seth, and then I'd remember. I'd put my hair up, and I'd remember again. I'd think about what I was doing next weekend and the weekend after that and the weekend after that. I'd remember and forget and remember and forget.

It was like my brain was still trying to process what happened, so I had to relive it over and over again.

I played all my Seth memories in my head like a photo stream from someone's vacation.

It was just last Friday, eight days ago, when we went to the duck pond after school. We stopped at his house on the way so he could pick up leftover challah to throw in. "Those ducks are hungry and they deserve the good stuff," he explained to me on the drive over. "I've seen people throw in old matzoh. Can you believe that? The ducks don't want your old matzoh, people!"

I laughed. "Imagine if the ducks could write Yelp reviews."

When we got to the duck pond, we sat on the bench, right by the edge. Seth's arm was around me, and I rested my head on his chest. He kissed the top of my head. The sun was in my eyes and I'd forgotten my sunglasses, so he let me borrow his Yankees hat. It smelled like sweat and chlorine, but I didn't mind. I wanted to wear it forever.

"What do you think ducks talk about?" he asked when we were standing by the edge of the pond. "They're fully communicating right now through quacks. And it sounds important."

I threw in a mushed-up piece of challah. "I don't know," I said. "Arguments over who gets the most crumbs? Unrequited duck love?" I shrugged.

He pulled me in close and swiveled the brim of his hat around to the back so he could get a better angle. And then he kissed me, right there.

"You're so cute, Mia," he said, moving back for a second. "And you don't even realize it."

Seth Manzell thought *I* was cute.

Justine drove into the driveway, and I was grateful that her house was our sleepover place. She had the bigger room, and her own bathroom. I had to share with my dad. He always got toothpaste on the sink; he rarely remembered to clean it up.

I couldn't stomach the thought of facing him tonight, of telling him that Seth and I had broken up. My sadness was more than enough; I couldn't handle my dad's sadness too.

We went right upstairs and in the safety of Justine's room, everything felt a tiny bit better. We changed into pajamas and sprawled out on her bed.

"I can't believe this is how the night turned out for us," Justine said. "I know this isn't about me, but I was supposed to be making out with Julian Glazer right now."

"Yeah, when I couldn't sleep last night, I was daydreaming about you guys falling in love," I admitted. "We were going to spend all summer together, the four of us. The Fearsome Foursome or something."

I didn't know why I was saying any of this out loud.

As I talked, the painful reality sank in.

It stung.

No Seth. No Us.

No Julian and Justine.

Seth and I had plans, things we were going to do together. We were supposed to be snuggled close on a blanket at the Fourth of July fireworks; we were supposed to master piggyback rides in the pool.

Remember? Remember all these things we were going to do?

It felt like someone had snatched a beach blanket out from under me while I was still sitting on it. And now I had sand in my underwear.

Having Seth for a boyfriend meant that I wasn't as invisible. I'd go into senior year and actually feel like a person. Someone people knew. Same for Justine and Alexis. One boyfriend in the group meant that the others could have boyfriends eventually too. And we'd be something. We'd have status.

But not anymore. All of that had evaporated.

"Mia, I have to tell you something." Justine ran her words together and sat up against her pillows. "I am so sorry to be the one to tell you, but you might find out, and I just have to—"

"What is it?" I shrieked. "You're freaking me out." I inched away from her on the bed.

"I saw Seth making out with Adia at the party," she said. "When I went to pee. They were behind the grill."

"What?" I felt like someone had slapped me. "I saw them walking away from there together. But making out? For real?"

She scrunched up her face like she was in pain. "I couldn't believe it when I saw it, and at first I thought they were just talking super close, or maybe someone dared them to kiss, like just being dumb [illegible]" She looked away from me and twisted a curl around her finger.

"He hooked up with another girl at the party I was at and then broke up with me!" I screamed. I walked across the room, curled up on Justine's window seat, and covered my face with the pillow. "How could he do that?"

"I shouldn't have told you," Justine said, walking over. "I am so mad that he did this." She looked up at the faded glow-in-the-dark stars on her ceiling. "At a party? Where everyone was gonna see and find out, like, right away?"

"Adia Montgomery! She knew I was going out with him, too. . . . And what about Trent?"

Justine raised her eyebrows. "I don't know. I didn't see Trent, actually. I guess they're over?"

I rested my head on her shoulder. "Thank God we don't have to see any of these people all summer. Maybe they'll forget by the time school starts."

"Yeah, and you're not gonna have much time to think about it anyway," she added in her take-charge, Justine way. "We start work Monday. We're gonna be busy."

"Work? You really call what we're going to be doing work?" I laughed.

Justine's lottery-winning uncle had finally decided to pursue his lifelong passion and open up a snow cone shop. Only snow cones. Different flavors. Different toppings. Mix-ins, too. But no ice cream.

Simply Snow Cones: that was his business model and the name of the company.

We were going to be working with his stepson, Justine's step-cousin, Dennis.

I saw Dennis every summer at Justine's family barbecues. We never really talked; he was just there, like one of the outdoor chairs. The only real memory I have of him was when we were both at Justine's Bat Mitzvah. He was trying to get the band to enforce the rules of the limbo competition; so many little kids were cheating and not taking it seriously. Justine was really embarrassed, but I thought he was kind of funny.

"It *is* work, Mia," Justine insisted. "Uncle Rick cares about this business."

She covered her mouth. She was laughing too.

I nodded, but deep down it didn't matter how busy we'd be, I knew I'd still have time to think about Seth. Because it wasn't like I only thought about Seth when I had time. I thought about Seth always. It didn't matter if I had five tests to study for—I still thought about Seth. Even when my grandma was in the hospital and she had a hundred and two fever, and I was pretty worried—I still thought about Seth.

Thoughts of Seth had settled in the very front of my brain. Like they were downloaded onto the laptop of my mind. Saved to the desktop.

One memory after another.

They weren't going anywhere.

It was going to be a long summer.

A long forever, it seemed like.

We slept in Justine's double bed, side by side, like hot dogs on a grill. At two in the morning, I woke up out of a sound sleep.

Justine was sitting on her bathroom floor, whispering into the phone.

I stayed still. Quiet.

"I mean, how could he do that to her?" Justine said. "And, like, I know this is selfish, but it's going to take her forever to get over this, and I don't want to spend all summer with a depressed mope. Can't you just bail on your dad? Come home, please."

Alexis.

The third person in our little trio. I guess you could consider us a trio, but when you broke it down, we were really a duo—Justine and Mia, with Alexis on the side.

That sounded mean—like she was a few mediocre crinkle-cut fries next to a delicious, buttery lobster roll.

We loved Alexis. We really did. But she wasn't around much. Her parents had split custody during the year, so she spent weekends with her dad, and summers, too. She was already at his summer home in the Catskills and wouldn't be back until the end of August.

"I never told you this, but I overheard his friends talking about her once," Justine whispered. "They were all at their lockers, and they were like, *Dude, she's kind of thick. Are you into thick girls?* They all started laughing and hitting each other. It was so gross. I mean, Mia's not even fat! So what if she's not emaciated like Laurel Peck, who looks like she's barely surviving a famine! What is wrong with people?"

Justine was quiet, listening to whatever Alexis was saying.

"As soon as Seth knew I overheard, he elbowed them, and they all shut up," Justine added. "But that doesn't change what they said. He sucks. So do his friends."

My heart sank to my toes.

"And Adia Montgomery. Come on. Ew." Justine groaned. "How could he do this to her?"

It was hard only hearing one end of the call. It was hard hearing the truth.

"I know that, Alexis. I know people break up all the time," she said. "But this just feels different. What he did is beyond the pale."

I looked at the clock on Justine's cable box. 2:07 AM.

And that's when I decided: I was done being chubby.

Done forever.

I could be a skinny girl if I tried hard enough. Anyone could.

There had to be a way to do it that was smart and sensible. So maybe I'd be a little bit hungry sometimes. I could handle it.

I turned onto my side and tried to fall back to sleep.

LIFE'S A BEACH

Cantaloupe, coconut, mango, peach, orange sorbet

JUSTINE

"We're going to the beach," I told Mia the next morning. "The ocean air always helps."

She sat up groggily, rubbing her eyes. "Okay."

"Just throw on your bathing suit from yesterday, and we'll get bagels on the way," I instructed. "Iced coffees, too. And let's go to Dream Beach, where we can rent the lounges and umbrellas."

"Okay," Mia said again, but she didn't move to get ready.

"Come on," I whined.

Maybe I was being too hard on her, rushing her too much. But we had one free day before work started, and I wanted to make the most of it.

Mia stayed quiet the whole ride to the bagel store.

"I'll wait in the car," she said when we got there, which sort of made sense because there were rarely any parking spots downtown, but it also felt lazy and gloomy. "Egg bagel scooped out with low-fat cream cheese and tomato. Skim in my iced coffee. Please. Thank you."

"Scooped out?" I exclaimed. "Who are you, Laurel Peck? Come on, Mi."

"Justine, it's not a big deal." She rolled her eyes. "I'm too tired to argue."

So I listened to her and got her what she wanted. Maybe this was part of her process, part of her healing.

I got back out to the car with the bagels and the coffees and found Mia singing loudly with the windows open.

"*Time casts a spell on you, but you won't forget me. I know I could have loved you . . . ,*" she sang like she was performing for thousands of people.

"What are you listening to?" I asked her, putting the iced coffees in the cup holders.

"A breakup songs playlist I found on Apple Music," she explained. "This is Fleetwood Mac. Awesome, right?"

"Turn it up," I said.

Mia sang the whole way to the beach. The windows were open, and the ocean air felt sticky and salty, like it was going to envelop us and heal all our wounds.

We ate our bagels and sipped our iced coffees and stared out into the sea.

"It's so worth it to rent these chairs," I said. "Don't you think? I mean, a lounge chair at the beach is always the way to go."

"Always," Mia said. "And I love how they have the terry covers for the cushions and the way they roll up the little towel at the end of the chair."

"Do you think other people appreciate good beach seating as much as we do?" I asked her, propping myself up on my elbow.

"Doubt it. The Skinnies always post pictures of themselves in bikinis on towels, flat on the sand," Mia said. "How can that be comfortable?"

"It's definitely not comfortable." I lay back down and then my phone rang, jolting me out of my blissful oceanside lounge-chair peace.

"Hi, Mom," I said, forcing myself to not sound annoyed.

"Where are you, Justine? You didn't say goodbye."

"I'm at the beach with Mia. I told you we were going," I explained. "I'll be home later."

"I would've come to the beach," she replied.

"Okay, Mom. We'll go together another day." I felt little pinches in my heart, slimy guilt that my mom was home doing nothing.

We hung up and I flipped onto my side to face Mia. "My mom wanted to come to the beach with us."

"She could've come."

"Mia! No!" I flipped the other way.

Why couldn't my mom have her own friends? Other moms played cards or went out to ladies' lunches or volunteered. I was my mom's favorite person, and that was exhausting.

"It's, like, when you look at the ocean, you realize your problems are all really small," Mia said, pulling me out of my guilt. "Ya know? Like we're all part of this vast universe."

I nodded, folding my arms behind my head. "Totally. That's why people who live on the beach are way happier."

"Is that a scientific fact?" Mia asked, giggling.

"I think so. Google it."

"See those rocks over there?" Mia pointed. "That's where Seth and I sat the night we came here. It was so dark, but he brought a flashlight."

"Sounds hot," I said, rubbing more sunscreen on my legs. The way she talked, it sounded like Seth was still hers, like they were still a thing. I wasn't sure if I should drag her out of denial or let her stay there for a little while longer.

"I want to go back to that moment," she said. "Like, really badly. I wish in life you could just bounce yourself from one time to another time, back and forth. When you really missed something, you could just go back and visit it. Even for a second."

"Me too," I said, staring into the sea.

She crossed and uncrossed her legs. "I don't need to change things or, like, redo the past. I just want to go back and spend a little more time in the happy moments, ya know?"

"I know." I sipped my iced coffee. "Do you think we are the way we are because of what happened to us? Or because we were just born a certain way?"

Mia crinkled her face. "What d'you mean? I don't get it."

"Just, like, are we who we are because of our upbringing, or were we destined to be the way we are?" I asked.

"I think it's both," Mia declared. "But I don't know."

I shrugged.

"The beach always brings out the introspection in people," Mia continued. "Seth and I had this whole conversation about birth order and if it makes a difference in your personality."

I dug my toes in the sand. "I wonder about that too."

"It's all just theories," Mia said. "We'll never really know."

"It seems like the more we know, the less we know." I laughed. "Ya know?"

"I know." She laughed too. "Seth thinks we're all just on this earth to make up for someone else's mistakes. . . ." She went on and on, and I let her talk as much as she wanted to.

I stared out into the ocean and tried to make all the problems seem as small as possible.

I LOVE YOU BERRY MUCH

Blueberries, raspberries, strawberries, almond milk

MIA

My dad drove us to the snow cone shop on the way to work the next morning. Normally Justine would be able to take the car, but she'd said the brakes felt weird on the way back from the beach yesterday. So it had to go to the mechanic. Her dad took the train to work, but her mom needed a car even though she rarely left the house. So we were carless for the day. Not that we really needed to get anywhere.

Life was so weird like that. You wanted things you didn't need. And when you had things you needed, you never appreciated them until they were gone.

Justine's ability to drive us to work was never a big deal before. She drove us to school every day, and I only appreciated it half of the time—like on the days we picked up bagels.

But now, without that car, I felt even more devastated than I'd felt before. Like that car was the only thing keeping me going, the only thing that would get me through the day.

"Good luck, girls," my dad said. He raised his eyebrows at me as I unbuckled my seat belt. That was his signature farewell. His facial expressions pretty much all said the same thing: *I don't understand you. I'll keep trying.*

"Bye, Dad."

"Thanks, Mr. Remsen," Justine said as she got out of the car.

My dad wasn't the kind of guy who insisted on being called by his first name, or joked around that Mr. Remsen was actually his father. He just went along, quietly, through the world, not making many waves. He didn't really get flustered, but he didn't get excited, either.

We walked into the shop, and Justine's uncle was there, doing something on the computer.

He threw his hands in the air. "You're here! Hurray!"

He's crazy, Justine mouthed to me.

Truthfully, he never seemed *that* crazy. He was Justine's mom's little brother, and he was always doing wacky things. Buying businesses, selling businesses, moving to California, moving to Japan. Moving back to Connecticut. But he always seemed happy. Happier than any of the adults I knew. I guess that's what happens when you win the lottery. You're happy.

Happy and a little bit crazy.

"Let's get started. I'll teach you everything you need to know in five minutes. Who has a stopwatch?" He winked at me.

Justine scoffed, "No one wears watches anymore, Uncle Rick. Come on."

"Oh." He laughed. "Little Justine, keeping me on my toes. Right, Mia? Right?"

"Right," I said, forcing a smile.

He showed us where the scoopers were, how to make sure the freezer door was properly closed. He showed us how to use the cash register and the credit card swipe machine. How to lock the shop at the end of the day.

"You're all set," he said.

"I think I got it all, but if we forget something, can we text you?" I asked him.

"Yessirree. Of course. I'm a very good texter." He patted us both on the backs. "You'll be fine, girls. By the way, Dennis won't be in today, but he'll be here tomorrow."

It was a little weird that Dennis was missing the first day of work, but I was grateful not to have to make conversation with him. My mind was too clogged with Seth thoughts to talk to people.

"And one more thing," Rick said on his way out. "I bought a van, too. So we'll have a permanent shop and a mobile shop." He stopped to think for a second. "I shouldn't call it a van—maybe it's a truck? Food trucks are the new thing, right?"

We nodded.

"Since he's my stepson and I'm trying to get the guy to like me, I asked Dennis which he'd prefer—shop or truck—and he picked shop . . . so you guys will be handling the truck."

"For real?" Justine perked up. "Uncle Rick, you're cooler than I thought you were."

"Why, thank you." He took an over-the-top bow. "Anyway, just putting some final touches on the truck. So get ready for it tomorrow!"

"Okay!" Justine clapped. "Wait! I have a name for it!"

"A name?" Uncle Rick turned around.

"Mobile Cones! Mobile Cones!" Justine shimmied. "Please paint that on the side of the truck."

Uncle Rick thought about it for a second and then agreed.

Justine high-fived me.

"Snow cone truck! Food truck! Hello?" Justine yelped as soon as Uncle Rick was out of the shop. "This is freaking cool! I never expected this."

"Um, yeah, I guess. . . ." My voice trailed off.

"Mia." She put her hands on my shoulders and stared into my eyes. "I know you're too sad to see anything good right now. But this is great. This means freedom for us! We won't be stuck in this shop all day."

"Uh-huh." I guess nothing would have made me happy right then. Also, I'd had five blueberries and a cheese stick for breakfast. I was starving.

Operation Skinny was off to a miserable start.

I looked at the clock. 9:53 AM.

Time seemed to be moving backward. Making it through the hours to when I'd be brushing my teeth and crawling into bed felt impossible.

"Wait, how much money did Uncle Rick win?" I asked Justine, staring out the window.

"Like forty-six million or something." She plopped down in a wheelie desk chair and scratched a mosquito bite on her arm. "But ya know, with taxes and stuff . . . who knows how much they really keep."

"So basically money buys happiness?" I asked her. "He's, like, the happiest guy ever."

"Nah," she said. "But it helps."

I tried to think of anything I could to avoid thinking about Seth. I organized the big jugs of mix-ins in the back. I spritzed the counter. I wiped the counter. I doodled little hearts on a pad of paper I found in the drawer.

Nothing helped.

"You're thinking about him again, aren't you?" Justine stared at her phone.

"No," I lied.

"Yes, you are." She put her phone down on the counter and glared at me. "What do you think Seth is even doing right now? Nothing cool, I'm sure."

I picked at my split ends. "How do you know?"

"Did he do anything *that* cool when you were together?" she pressed.

"Umm, when we got a flat on the way to Mr. Aja's end-of-the-year party, he changed the tire himself," I said, feeling oddly proud. "He actually reads the books in English, and he can make fresh whipped cream, and he's been to like thirty Phish shows."

"Um, no," Justine scoffed. "Going to Phish shows doesn't make you cool."

"Okay, Justine." I went back to doodling.

She kicked my chair a little so it wheeled in her direction. "And the rest of it? So what? Snooze fest."

"Fine. I don't need to convince you," I said. I kept hearing *she's thick* again and again. It stung. But I couldn't stop the echo.

I thought of him and Adia walking out from behind that grill. He'd kissed her like he kissed me. His hands on her cheeks like they'd been on mine. His lips on her lips.

He was a sleazebag, and I hated him. But I still wanted him to be mine. I still wanted him to love me.

She stared at me silently for a few moments and then she said, "No. I need to convince you."

SOUL CLEANSER

Swiss chard, spinach, mango, rice milk

JUSTINE

"V/NV," I said to Mia, who was just sitting there in the snow cone shop, staring at a pen in her hand. "Soleil Mateno. Go."

"I don't feel like playing," Mia said under her breath.

"Come on. Please," I begged. I didn't know why I loved this game so much. It was noon on our first day of work, and we hadn't had any customers yet. But snow cones weren't really a morning treat. It would be better when we were in the truck.

"NV. She's, like, gorgeous. And remember she told us how she fell in love with that boy in Tulum when she was on vacation with her family last winter? I bet they did it on the beach at sunset." Mia looked up at me finally. "Happy?"

"Fine." I looked at her sad, droopy green eyes. It seemed like tears were piling up behind them, ready to pour out like the bucket at the top of a water slide. I wished I could wipe it all away, erase that any of it happened. Or at least do something to make her feel better.

I tapped her knee. "Why are you staring at that pen? What is the deal with that pen?"

"Huh?" Mia quickly put it in her pocket.

"Mia." I swiveled my chair closer to hers. "Talk to me. I'm worried."

She rolled her lips together. "Seth gave me this pen." She took it out again. "See how it says BRIDGEFIELD ESTATES? His mom is on the zoning board." She started to cry.

"When did he give you the pen?" I tried to ask with a straight face, take her seriously, and sound sympathetic.

"One day in assembly. We had to choose our electives." She sobbed. "I didn't have a pen and he gave it to me, and he never asked for it back."

I moved closer and put my arms around her. "It's gonna be okay, Mi." She stayed in the hug, and I felt little teardrops on my shoulder. "I promise. It's gonna be okay."

We sat in silence for a while and then Mia said, "Seth's probably at the pool with Adia right now."

"Uh-huh," I said, scrolling through Instagram, trying to find some quote that would help her. "But maybe he's not. Maybe he's, like, at the podiatrist because he has some mystery fungus growing on his toenail."

"What?" Mia cracked up.

"Like a really gross one that changes colors, and now his toe is so swollen that he can't even walk anymore," I continued.

Mia pulled the hood of her sweatshirt down over her face. "Okay, I get it. I'll stop talking about him."

"Let's do something," I said, grabbing her hand so she would stand up. She followed me to the back of the shop and we looked at all the jugs of snow cone flavoring.

"Uncle Rick is so basic," I continued. "I mean, peach, coconut, mango—does he expect everyone to order just one flavor?"

Mia shrugged, like she was only half paying attention.

"And why is orange the only cream pop flavor?" I asked her. "Doesn't a blueberry cream pop sound so good?"

"Yeah, sure," she answered, staring at her phone.

I sighed and looked over her shoulder at the cheesy quote Instagram account she was following.

Those who do not know how to weep with their
whole heart do not know how to laugh either.
—Golda Meir

"What?" She looked up at me. "I'm weeping with my whole heart. And Golda Meir gets it."

Operation Cheer Up Sad Mia was going to be a tough one, but I was going to do it.

"Okay, put down the phone and close your eyes," I said, leading her to a stool to sit down. "I'm going to combine three flavors and pour them onto the ice, and you have to guess what they are!"

"Okay," she said.

"Oh! And we'll name them after people from school!" I shouted as I mixed. "How funny will that be?"

"Only if you make the Adia the grossest flavor possible," she replied.

"Well, duh." I poured on the flavors and then walked over with the finished snow cone. I tapped her hand. "Try this. Keep your eyes closed so the colors don't give anything away."

Mia opened her mouth and took a tiny bite of the icy mixture. "Um," she said, raising her eyebrows. "Pineapple, orange, root beer? No offense, but it tastes kind of gross, like half-sweet, half-bitter."

"That was intentional." I nodded, laughing. "It's the Laurel Peck!"

Mia shook her head, but she was giggling a little too. "Oh, Laurel's not *that* bad! Were my flavors right?"

"The root beer yes, the others no—it was pomegranate, rhubarb, and root beer," I explained. "Rhubarb, Uncle Rick? Come on!"

"Okay, my turn!" Mia got up from the chair. "No peeking!"

I hopped up onto the counter and smiled when her back was to me. She was cheering up, just the littlest bit. Maybe she'd make it through this. With my help, and the comic relief of an only-snow-cone shop, she'd be able to survive.

"Justine! Eyes closed!" she yelled back to me.

I kept seeing the Adia/Seth behind-the-grill scene in my head. I didn't want to, but it would just sort of appear. If that was happening to me, how could I blame Mia for thinking about it?

What was wrong with him? You'd have to be a complete sleazebag to do something like that. Unless Adia had cornered him, and she was like, *It's my party. I can kiss who I want to.* And Seth didn't have a choice.

Was that possible? Nah. We always had a choice.

"Okay! Go!" Mia tapped the snow cone against my lips and I took a bite.

"Ack, Mi, what's in this?" I stuck my tongue out. "I need water."

She handed me my Poland Spring, and when I was finally able to talk again I said, "Um, cinnamon, sour grape, and jalapeño?"

She cracked up. "How did you get that totally right? Did you get a flavor list in advance or something?"

"Just a good guess." I chugged the rest of my water. "That was disgusting. Really and truly. And hot."

"Exactly." She smiled. "I call it the Seth."

I wanted to throw something at her. "Mia!"

She slumped down. "I just want to know what he's doing right now," she admitted. "I know it's pathetic. But I want to know. I can't stand not talking to him. I keep checking to see if he's posted anything new, but nothing. He's probably with Adia, making out on a lounge by her pool." She stuck her tongue out like she was about to throw up.

"Let's go see if he's there," I said. "We'll come right back in case there are customers. Then you'll know what he's doing and you can stop wondering. I guess sometimes you just have to face things head-on."

"You don't have your car today, remember?" Mia reminded me.

"Right. Duh. Okay, tomorrow then." A lightbulb went on in my brain. "In our SNOW CONE TRUCK!" I screamed.

A magical, innocent, perfect way to stalk Seth.

No one would recognize us!

Mia gave me a halfhearted thumbs-up while staring at her phone.

"You're still studying Seth's Facebook profile, searching for clues?" I asked her, hopping down from the counter to make some more concoctions.

Mia rolled her eyes. That was exactly what she was doing, and I knew it.

"What do you think you're going to find out?" I asked her. "Staring at it, waiting for him to post something . . . I mean, what's the point?"

"He just posted some article about the coach of the Villanova basketball team." She shrugged, acting like she didn't care, but I knew she was reading the article like it was the most interesting thing in the world. She was probably ordering a Villanova hoodie right now. "I just want to know what he's thinking, why he did what he did. It's so unfair that I don't get to know, that I can't find out."

I walked over to her. "Why aren't you madder? Like, aren't you so pissed that this stupid boy could break your heart like this?" I asked. "Be mad. Come on."

"He's on Facebook Messenger, though," she said, completely ignoring me. "I didn't even know he used that."

"Mia!" I shouted. "Seriously?"

That's when it hit me: I couldn't simply be a bystander at the crime scene of Mia's obsession. If I had to be a part of it, I had to be an active part of it.

I was her best friend. It was basically my job to help her. I couldn't let Mia do this to herself.

Some people say that the best revenge is success, and maybe that's true. But success can take a while.

So the backup plan: regular revenge.

We could hurt Seth like he had hurt her. Just in our own way.

"Come here, let me see," I said.

"See what? Seth's Facebook page? Aren't you his friend?" Mia's eyes lit up. Like she was already happier just because I was talking about Seth, and not just uh-huhing and nodding.

"I am his friend." I smiled. "But we're going to be making him a *new* friend."

"Huh?" Mia took a sip of the strawberry-mango-pineapple slushie concoction I'd made when I blended the ice for too long.

Uncle Rick was committed to an only-snow-cone shop. He'd reminded us of that over and over again, but slushies were kind of like snow cones, just mushed up.

It got me thinking—we're different versions of ourselves, depending on who we're talking to and what we're doing.

Sometimes we're a snow cone, sometimes we're a slushie. Maybe that's not such a bad thing.

💔 💔 💔

"Who's Katie McCormick?" Mia scoffed, reading over my shoulder.

"She sounds like a real person, right?" My heart pounded.

"Um, I guess so," Mia replied, confused.

"She's from Easterly." The more I said about Katie, the more real she felt. She was a Polaroid picture in my hands, coming into focus.

I'd spent my sixteen years of life wishing my parents were different. Why did they have to argue so much? Why couldn't they just talk like normal people?

It was a waste of time. Complete and total waste.

Wishing and hoping wouldn't change them.

But now, this was my chance!

Forget about change—I could create a whole person. To be exactly the way I wanted her to be. She'd be able to find out everything Mia ever wanted to know about Seth! Why he broke up with her, what happened that night, why he hooked up with Adia.

And then: we'd embarrass him way worse than he'd embarrassed her.

"What are you doing?" Mia asked, leaning over my shoulder. "You look like some kind of mad scientist, mixing potions in test tubes, waiting for an explosion."

"I feel like that, actually! And I love it."

"You're freaking me out," Mia continued.

I looked up from the computer. "Do you think Katie's a softball player? Or soccer? Or maybe she does some kind of modern dance? Plays the cello? Mathletes?"

Mia closed the computer. "Seriously. Stop."

"What? Why?"

"We're not doing this," Mia insisted. "This is not how we're spending our summer. Sitting in a snow cone shop, making up a fake person so we can stalk my ex-boyfriend. Please. We're better than this."

Mia went on and on, like she was reading a script. There was no emotion in her voice; I knew she was just saying what she thought she was supposed to say.

"Fine. If you don't mention Seth for the rest of the day, I'll pretend Katie doesn't exist," I told her. I was setting my best friend up for failure. But truthfully, I knew my plan would benefit her in the long run.

"She *doesn't* exist!" Mia laughed. "Justine, seriously. I know you're bored, but you're taking things too far."

I pshawed her and waved a hand in her face. "I haven't done anything yet. Calm down."

Later that afternoon, a few kids came by on their way home after a soccer game. They were sweaty and smelled bad, and they wanted to sample every flavor before they decided on one. But they were still paying customers.

"If you were just a little closer to the field, you'd have tons of business," the mom told us.

I told her about the truck. I took a screen shot of the map of the field she was talking about.

"We'll be there tomorrow," I said. "Look for the truck that says Mobile Cones."

💔 💔 💔

Mia failed at her mission. She couldn't make it to the end of the day without mentioning Seth. She couldn't even make it a whole hour without mentioning Seth.

I wasn't surprised. And I'll admit: I was happy about this. I wanted to create Katie. I wanted to do something.

So much of life was sitting and waiting for something to happen. You couldn't control other people and you couldn't make them change. You could only change yourself, your attitudes, how you responded to others.

But that seemed like a load of crap to me. It didn't seem like enough.

Mia was sleeping over. We had a whole evening in front of us to figure out who Katie McCormick really was, and how she'd found her way to Seth Manzell.

It was time to get to work.

FLAX YOUR MUSCLES

Celery, flaxseed, blueberries, almond milk, spinach

MIA

I failed on purpose. Well, not exactly on purpose. But I knew I wouldn't be able to succeed. Talking about Seth was my only way to make sense of what had happened. And honestly, I loved talking about him. He still felt mine, in some small way.

He was actually a boy who liked me, not one I just daydreamed about liking me. Not one I obsessed over from afar.

I loved the voice mails he'd leave me: *Hey, Mia. It's me, Seth.* Not *It's Seth.* He added *me.* I liked that. It felt special. Maybe he said that on everyone's voice mail, but it felt like he only said it on mine.

And when I got the flu in February, he came over anyway. He brought me chicken soup from the deli in town. He sat with me watching shows on Bravo all day long. He didn't mind the piles of wadded-up tissues on the coffee table.

Out of all the girls in school, Seth Manzell picked *me.*

But that was over now. Five months of bliss: over. I couldn't handle it. I missed Seth. I missed having a boyfriend; I missed being part of a couple. What if I never had it again?

Justine and I sat side by side at her desk. "Okay. So far we have that Katie McCormick lives in Easterly and she likes modern dance." She folded her hands in her lap and looked at me wide-eyed. "And?"

I leaned back in my chair. "I still don't really understand what this Katie McCormick person is supposed to do. I mean, we can see Seth's Facebook page ourselves. Same with Twitter, Instagram, whatevs. What can Katie McCormick do that we can't do?"

"Just trust me," Justine said. "You'll see what she can do when she starts doing it."

I swallowed hard.

"Also, it's not only about what Katie can do. It's about what Seth will do," Justine added.

"Uh-huh." Clearly Justine had a plan, but I didn't understand why she was being so vague about it. I wanted to ask questions, but I was too scared of the answers.

"We're going to make Seth fall in love with Katie," Justine said, like it was the simplest thing in the world. "And then crush him completely. I'm talking gut-wrenching pain, here."

There was passion in her scheming.

"Also, how many times have we wondered what guys thought?" she asked me. "Like about anything. Girls, hooking up, life . . . they're so mysterious. Now we can find out everything we've ever wanted to know." She bulged out her eyes. "Mia! This is huge!"

"Okay, okay, I get it." I laughed.

"But the thing is, he's pathetic, but he's not literally the most pathetic person in the world, to fall in love with some complete stranger who found him online. So we're going to need to do some digging," Justine explained.

I wanted to stop her. I wanted to tell her to stop calling Seth pathetic. I was angry that he'd broken up with me, but I still loved him. I still desperately wished he'd change his mind. I wished he'd tell me this was all a mistake, that he wanted to be back together.

But this little experiment of Justine's was all I had left of him. So I didn't stop her. As long as we were doing this, it was okay for me to think about him all the time.

"So it says here he's a part of this Connecticut Teens Volunteer Corps." Justine pointed to the computer. "Katie needs to join that."

Justine clicked the Join Group tab and voilà, just like that Katie McCormick was a volunteer.

"Um, she doesn't have any photos," I reminded Justine. "She's this blank person without any friends who just joined Facebook. This doesn't seem believable."

"Relax. Please." Justine sat back in her chair and stayed quiet for a little while, thinking.

"What are you going to do?" I asked. "Make up a million fake friends for her? Find some random photos? Justine, seriously. Let's be done. This is really crazy. We're the pathetic ones."

She didn't answer me. Within five minutes she was on the phone with her cousin Lara in California. She explained the whole thing. They were going to unfriend each other. And then Katie was going to friend all of Lara's friends. On and on and on. They had a plan.

I had a million explanations for why Justine was so committed to doing this. One was that she really did want to help me get over Seth. Fine. Simple enough. She hated what he'd done to me as much as I hated it. So revenge was a big part of it.

But the other reasons were deeper: I always believed Justine wanted to be a different person, have different parents, lead a different life. Maybe this was her chance? I wasn't a psychologist, obviously, but there was something else to her passionate, very crazy mission.

I just hadn't figured it out yet.

CASHEW NEW YOU

Cashew butter, coconut milk, strawberries, pineapple

MIA

I woke up starving at six in the morning. The only thing I wanted in the entire world was for Seth Manzell to love me again . . . and an egg-and-cheese sandwich.

I left Justine a note that I would be back in plenty of time for work, and I tiptoed down the creaky front stairs, and out of her house, and started the short trek into town. I mean, I was walking there and back, so that would pretty much cancel out most of the calories from the egg-and-cheese. I didn't need to diet *all* the time.

It felt like the whole world was still asleep, except for the commuters going to the train station. In a way, it was nice to be up this early. Like I got a head start on the day. I was awake before anyone could bother me.

I was almost at Carlton's for the best egg-and-cheese on the planet, when someone bumped into me. "The line starts around the corner, at the end of Hemlock."

"Huh?" I asked. My sleepy town was suddenly crowded and moody.

"The line for Juiceteria," the woman said. "I figured that's why you were up this early. You know the new flavor comes out today."

"Um, okay." I peered around the corner. "Thanks."

"I heard this month's smoothie is their best yet. Something with pineapple . . . I mean, pineapple has all sorts of magical qualities. You know what they say about pregnant women—" She was interrupted by a gaggle of middle-aged women who arrived to join her. Apparently she was saving a space for them in line.

I still wanted the egg-and-cheese, but something told me to wait on the line.

A crowd at six-thirty in the morning? In Bridgefield?

Magical qualities of pineapple.

I couldn't ignore all that.

CHEER-UP CHERRY

Cherries, soy milk, wheatgrass, blueberries, kale

JUSTINE

"We need to make one stop," Mia told me as soon as we were in my car, on the way to pick up the truck.

"Where?" I asked, turning up the AC.

"Juiceteria," she said. "It opened up last year, I think. There was a line around the corner this morning, and I totally get it. It's amazing. It's like dieting without torture. That should be their slogan."

I nodded. "It does sound pretty good." I flipped through the radio stations, trying to find something that would wake me up. "But you were already there and you want to go back? Is it a cult?"

Mia cracked up. "A healthy cult! Oh, and I want to get you one! Wanna know the best part?"

"What?" I laughed. It was nice to see her excited about something.

"The smoothies have names, and, like, you totally pick based on your mood!"

"Like the way we are with nail polish. This Love Every Minute polish I picked is totally coming true."

"Hmm." Mia smiled. "Can we make an Ex-Boyfriend Still Loves Me color?"

"I'm not even responding to that." I turned the music up even louder, and I stopped outside Juiceteria.

Twenty minutes later, Mia came out with one goopy, brown, sludgelike drink and one peachy one, a color very similar to my toe polish, as a matter of fact.

"This is for you," she said, handing me the orange cup. "Peach Perfect!" She giggled.

"Thanks, and what's that one?" I asked her, trying not to gag. It looked and smelled like the slop at the bottom of a Dumpster.

"The Cheer-Up Cherry."

"That is a good name, even if it smells disgusting. I guess you have to weigh the pros and cons." I tried my smoothie. "Ooh, this one's delish! Thank you!"

I rested it in the cup holder and started driving.

"The name just spoke to me. I mean, I definitely need cheering up. But the ingredients are good too: wheatgrass, blueberries, cherries, kale, soy milk . . ."

I reached my arm out for her to hand me the cup. "Not bad,"

I said after a sip. "It tastes better than it smells. I prefer the peach, though."

A few minutes later, we'd parked in the lot by the shop, and we were ready to start our first day in the Mobile Cones truck.

"I'm scared to really and truly stalk," Mia said. "What if Seth sees us?"

"He doesn't know there's a food truck," I reminded her. "Honestly, he probably forgot what we're even doing this summer. He doesn't pay attention."

"He does, sometimes," she defended him.

We drove for a few minutes and stopped halfway down the block from Seth's house. In all fairness, there was a park with a playground at the end of his street, and there were kids playing there, so it was a good location for a mobile snow cone shop to hunker down.

We sat back in our seats and put our feet up on the dashboard. The breeze was blowing in through the open windows. It was one of those perfect summer days where the air feels delicious, no humidity whatsoever.

I pulled up Katie's Facebook page on my phone and looked it over. Mia leaned in closer to get a better view.

"So we're in a food truck, looking at a fake person's Facebook page, stalking my ex-boyfriend," Mia announced.

"We are," I replied. "When you say it like that, it sounds sad. So please don't say it like that."

"Um, okay, let me rephrase." Mia laughed and sipped her smoothie. "We're snow cone saleswomen, creators of contemporary fictional characters, engaging in a social experiment about what it takes to get over a first love."

"Yes!" When she put it that way, it did sound pretty good.

"Before we broke up, I had all these fantasies about Seth picking me up from work at the end of the day, and us, like, making out in the giant freezer," Mia said, taking her feet down from the dashboard. "Doesn't that sound hot?"

I rolled my eyes. "Well, it sounds freezing, actually, but yeah, also hot."

"And he'd be our taste tester, and I'd feed him snow cones. . . ."

"He wouldn't have time for all that; he's too busy *volunteering,*" I mocked.

"People make time for hooking up in a freezer."

I lowered the music and turned to face her. "I mean, what's so douchey about Seth is that he volunteers and he's all high-and-mighty about it. But like, he only does it for college. So wouldn't it be way less douchey if he didn't volunteer at all?" I rambled on. "He's just so phony."

"We're all a little phony," Mia replied. "I pretend I love snow cones when I'm talking to the customers, but obviously regular ice cream is way better."

"That's your job," I reminded her. "It's different."

"Sit back, sit back!" Mia screeched, looking through the mirror on her side.

I glanced up through the rearview and saw Seth leaving his house. He had a backpack over both shoulders and his worn-out Yankees hat on.

I hated that hat.

Mia talked through her teeth. "Justine, come on. He's going to see us!"

She was scared and happy at the same time, and at that moment I wondered if we should stop. Maybe I was prolonging the agony. But I had to believe that in the long run, it would be worth it. We couldn't let him get away with what he'd done.

"Calm down," I said. We were far enough that he wouldn't see us.

"So now what?" Mia asked me. "He got in his car and left."

"Right," I said.

"And?"

"And we want to get a sense of his schedule, so we know when Katie should start talking to him," I explained. "Please. Just let me be in charge."

"Aren't you always in charge?" Mia asked me.

She was right. I *was* always in charge. But that was our dynamic, the way it had been since kindergarten, and it was way too late to change it now.

"Come on," I said. "We have snow cones to sell."

RISE-UP RASPBERRY

Raspberry, mint, coconut water, watermelon, spinach

MIA

Alexis came home for two days, totally unexpectedly. Her dad had to go to a conference in Toronto, so she was back in Bridgefield staying with her mom.

Alexis's mom got remarried last summer to this guy Bernie. His shirts bulged in the middle, he sweat when he ate, and he drooled when he got really fired up about something. His wife died six years ago from brain cancer. It was pretty clear he wanted someone, anyone, to help run his life. Alexis's mom was good at stuff like that.

"We're friends because we all have problems with our moms," Alexis told her stepsister, Roey. She was eleven and very impressionable. Alexis was pretty dead set on corrupting her. We were sitting in their kitchen, picking at the remnants of an old birthday cake. "Hers is dead." She pointed to me. "Hers is crazy." She pointed to Justine. "And mine is—well, you know what mine is. A lovable control freak."

It was nice that she added the lovable part.

"Okay," Roey said. "But all that matters is that you guys are best friends. I hope I have friends like you guys when I'm in high school."

"You probably won't." Alexis rebutted Roey's dream. "We're pretty much one of a kind. But ya know, it's good that you have lofty aspirations. See ya, Ro. We got places to be!"

Roey flopped herself forward onto the kitchen island, deflated that we were leaving so quickly.

"You're so mean to her," I whispered once we were outside on the hammock. I had a feeling Roey was hiding somewhere, and I didn't want her to overhear me.

"So what? It'll make her tougher. She doesn't need to be such a wimpy little girl." Alexis groaned. "Anyway, enough about her. I was scheduled for a massage today and then my dad had to bounce to some conference, and now I'm back here with you losers."

Come to think of it, Alexis was mean to everyone. That was just her way: prickly and rough.

"What are you drinking?" Alexis made a face. "It smells like the organic floor cleaner my dad's cleaning lady uses."

"Huh?" I shook my head. "It's a smoothie."

"It looks really and truly disgusting."

"You don't know about Juiceteria either?" I squawked. "It's, like, the biggest thing in town. We are so out of it."

"The biggest thing in town," Justine mocked.

"It's called Rise-Up Raspberry, for when you really want to rise to the challenge of life," I explained. "Raspberry, mint, coconut water, watermelon, spinach."

Alexis looked like she was about to puke. She turned away from me and flicked Justine on the eyebrow. "Why aren't you guys at work?" Alexis asked. "Put down your phone already, Justine. I'm here for like a day. Come on."

"Stop," Justine whined. "You're so annoying."

"What are you doing on your phone all day anyway?" Alexis pressed. "You're being weird."

My heart thumped. Was Justine going to tell Alexis about our mission? I didn't want anyone else to know about it. It seemed like the more people who knew, the weirder and creepier it became.

Justine and I made eye contact. *Please don't tell her,* I pleaded.

"Nothing, sorry." Justine put her phone in the back pocket of her shorts.

Thank you, I mouthed to her. This was our thing. Our secret thing. Alexis didn't need to know.

Justine kept talking. "We're off today because Uncle Rick wasn't happy with the original paint job for the Mobile Cones truck. So he took it somewhere else. He thinks a prettier truck will sell more snow cones."

"I guess millionaires can afford to take risks," Alexis said. "And you girlies get to hang with me! Lucky!"

"Yippee." Justine forced excitement. "So what should we do? I'm not spending all day on your dilapidated hammock with Ro-Ro following us around."

"Sorry I'm not the entertainment committee you expected," Alexis mocked, and turned to me. "So you and Seth are still over?"

"Yup," I said, clumps forming in my throat. *Don't cry. Don't cry.*

"I guess I should tell you. . . ." She looked straight into my eyes. "He tried to make out with me once, grabbed my boobs and everything. I wasn't into it."

"What? When?" I sat up and nearly made the hammock tip over. "You didn't tell me!"

"Calm down. It was like a month before you guys started going out." She rolled her eyes. "We were putting our instruments away in the band room closet. And he was like, *The way you play your flute is so hot,* and I was like—"

Alexis burst out laughing so hard she stopped talking. I snatched the hammock pillow away from Justine and hit Alexis over the head with it again and again.

I was annoyed at Alexis for making up that lie and thinking I'd believe it, but it felt good to hit her with the pillow. It felt good to laugh.

"Sorry, Mia, your facial expression was just too good," Alexis said. "You looked like you were about to pass out. Didn't she, Justie?"

Justine deep-sighed. "You don't know the half of it. She carries around a pen he once lent her in assembly. She, like, holds it and stares at it and stuff."

"Wow." Alexis shook her head. "Mia, Mia, Mia. He's just not worth it."

Justine put an arm around me. "We'll help you through this,

Mi. But let's get out of here. Ro-Ro's staring at us from the window, and I feel guilty."

She had a soft spot for Roey. Justine had a much older half brother, from her dad's first marriage. He lived in San Francisco and she never saw him. She always wished for a younger sister.

Come to think of it, maybe that's why we were friends. It wasn't the mother thing. It was the sibling thing. All three of us were only children.

A stepsister here some of the time, a half brother far away all the time. They didn't really count.

We decided to go for frozen yogurt and then sit in the gazebo at Pebble Park.

I wanted chocolate fudge brownie in a sugar cone, but I was still pretty full from the smoothie and I wanted to be loyal to the Skinny Mission. I got cucumber water instead. I was midsip when Alexis said, "I know what you guys are doing."

My whole body tightened.

"You left your phone on the counter when you were digging through your bag to find your wallet so you could pay for the fro yo. You really need to clean that thing out. You can never find anything in that bag," she lectured Justine. "So. Katie McCormick?"

"Huh? Who's that?" Justine asked, all cool.

"Don't *who's that* me," Alexis warned.

Alexis knew. She knew everything.

"So Seth unfriended you guys after the breakup, and this is the only way you can figure out what he's doing?" she asked, like she'd figured it all out. "Lame. So lame. You're that desperate to know the stupid stuff Seth posts that you need to make up a freakin' fake person so you can anonymously online-stalk him?"

So she didn't know. Well, she knew a tiny little part of it, I guess. But she didn't know the whole thing. She didn't know what was really going to happen with Katie McCormick.

I was relieved and completely freaked out all at once.

BEETER THAN BEFORE

Beet greens, melon, rice milk, kiwi

MIA

"I don't understand the picture. . . . Who is that?" I shrieked to Justine over the phone later that night.

"Okay, so there are these sites with, like, random photos of people. . . . I think they're used for magazines, maybe? Book covers? I don't even know." Justine crunched something; it sounded like a pretzel. "But she looks perfect, right? Like, pretty but not too pretty. She looks so much like Katie. She is Katie."

"Justine, seriously? This is sick."

"No, it isn't. It's just a photo. Calm down."

I sighed. "Do you even know what you're saying anymore?"

"Yes, I do." She paused. "I know exactly what I'm doing."

"Justine," I pressed.

"What? Please just trust me. I wouldn't do this if I didn't truly believe it was going to help you get over Seth." She crunched again.

"And also totally mess with him in a major way, something he'll never expect. We need to get back at him, Mia. You can't just go on feeling so sad. Revenge is the answer!"

The truth was, it was crazy and it was a bad idea. But we had already started it. And I did want to destroy him.

"So Uncle Rick has the truck back." Justine changed the subject. "We're all set for tomorrow."

"And what about Katie McCormick?" I asked.

"What about her?"

"Well, when does she start doing something? So far she's just the photos of a random girl with an interest in modern dance and volunteer work," I explained. "When is she actually going to talk to Seth?"

"Oh, just you wait," Justine said. "I'm still fine-tuning. We can't have her contact him too soon. We need to find her friends, more interests, an Instagram page that links to Facebook. She needs to take really artsy photos of lakes and woods and stuff. I think she's into hiking."

"Okay, but shouldn't I be part of the fine-tuning?" I asked her.

"You are," Justine replied, but then stopped suddenly. I heard yelling in the background. Her door closed. And then she sighed. "I gotta go, Mia. I'll text you when I'm on my way tomorrow."

I said goodbye, but I doubt she heard it. When the yelling started, Justine turned into some kind of ceramic statue.

Justine's parents were fighters, but when the arguments ended, everything went back to normal. It always seemed like everyone forgot about the fight. Like it would never happen again.

Justine had told me the password for Katie's Facebook page, but I hadn't gone on by myself yet. I guess it seemed safer when Justine was by my side. If I went on alone, I was really doing it. I was really a part of it, not just some innocent accomplice watching the whole thing.

But in the quiet of the night, I felt the need to log in by myself. I wanted to figure Katie out. I needed to add something to her story.

So I signed in. And there was her picture.

Whoever she was.

Katie could be anyone we wanted her to be. She could do anything we wanted her to do. She was putty in our hands, ready to be molded.

The more things I added, the more I wondered why it was so satisfying. Was it because I wanted to see what would happen? I was curious to find out if Seth would tell her things he'd never told me. Or maybe it was because I could create her; I could write her story.

Some of the things I decided on weren't even revealed on her Facebook page. Why would they be? Stuff about her family life. Stuff I so desperately wanted.

I imagined her, living in Easterly. A regular girl with a regular family.

She had a mom and dad who loved each other. A happy mom and a happy dad. They went out to dinner on Saturday nights; they really enjoyed each other's company.

And Katie had a little brother who played on the town soccer team. The whole family would go to watch his games on Sunday mornings. They'd pick up bagels on the way. They never restricted their carbs. They didn't need to.

Katie liked modern dance. And painting. She wanted to go to Oberlin. Or maybe Vassar. She wasn't quite sure yet. She dabbled in creative writing.

Katie volunteered at the local nursing home, playing cards with the residents every other Thursday. Her group of friends was popular, but not mean. They were all well liked. They stuck together. They did well in school. But they didn't spend their whole lives studying.

They were skinny, but not because they starved themselves.

Katie was everything extraordinary and yet so simple at the same time.

SURVIVAL

Almond butter, strawberries, banana, coconut, romaine

JUSTINE

"I did it," Mia said as she got in the car the next morning, before she even said hello.

"Did what?"

"I made some decisions for Katie . . . and then I wrote to Seth."

"What?" Katie was my creation. And now Mia was just going to jump in and make changes and make decisions without consulting me first?

"Wait, you're mad?" Mia asked me. "You gave me the password. I mean, isn't this all about me, anyway? I'm not allowed to be involved?"

I tried to stay calm. "No, you are. But it's just that . . . I figured you'd discuss it with me first. Like, we should be on the same page and stuff. Ya know?"

Mia glared at me. "Justine, seriously? You're getting a little crazy over this. Come on."

I *was* getting crazy over it. I was still all garbled up from my parents' fight. It was just their way of communicating, it happened all the time, but it still made me feel like I had rocks on my shoulders.

"So did Seth write back?" I asked her.

"Not yet." She scratched the top of her head.

When we got to the snow cone shop to pick up the truck, Mia showed me what she'd written.

> Hey. I saw you're on the list for the CT Volunteers Corps beach cleanup thingy on Saturday. We live kinda close to each other, so I figured I'd say hey. I'm Katie, by the way.

I looked at Mia. It was hard for me to admit this, since I had nothing at all to do with it, but it was good.

"Obviously she can't go to the beach cleanup," Mia said, like she had it all figured out. "But this is a way to get them talking."

She was right. "Good job, Mi-Mi." My insides felt fizzy.

Things were going to start happening. Now.

KIWI TO SUCCESS

Kiwi, papaya, Greek yogurt, dash of cayenne pepper

JUSTINE

"You're studying? In the summer?" I asked Dennis when we went into the shop on Saturday to get the keys to the truck. We'd decided it was safer to store them there than keep them with us overnight.

"Just a little side project of mine." He stared at his flash cards.

Side project?

"What is it?" Mia asked him.

I glared at her.

"Well . . ." He finally looked up at us. "Who was the losing vice-presidential candidate in 1952?"

"Ummmm . . . let me think about it," I replied. "Literally no idea whatsoever."

"John Sparkman," he said.

"Great. Good to know." I grabbed Mia's hand. "Come on. Let's go."

"Wait," Mia said, walking over to Dennis to look at his flash cards. "I don't get it. What is this?"

I put my hands on her shoulders to guide her over to the door, but she stayed put.

"I just think it would be cool if I knew all the losing vice-presidential candidates," he said, looking up at her. "Like for fun. A little trivia."

"How did you think of that?" Mia asked, genuinely interested.

Seriously, was she a journalist for the *Most Boring Things Ever Newspaper*? What was happening?

"I don't even know." He shrugged. "It just kind of came to me." He paused. "Actually, you guys can help quiz me!"

"No, thanks." I grabbed Mia's hand again. "We gotta go."

"All right, well, I'll be tweeting ya!" He laughed.

"Huh?" I turned around.

"Get it? Like I'll be seeing ya . . . but I'll be tweeting because, like, that's part of my job here."

Mia cracked up. "I get it."

"Well, thank goodness someone does." He went back to his flash cards. "See ya."

Uncle Rick had put Dennis in charge of all social media for the business. I was kind of shocked Uncle Rick even cared about social media, but he did. I was also kind of shocked that Dennis even knew what social media was.

"So we're just gonna show up at the volunteer thing?" Mia asked me once we were in the truck. She'd been sipping a bright orange smoothie all morning. Something with papaya. It smelled like a vegan's throw-up.

I nodded. "Yeah, we'll be there, and maybe some people will buy snow cones, and you'll be able to see that no one thinks Seth is cool whatsoever, and maybe he'll be looking for Katie, but she won't show up, and it'll be really funny to watch. . . ."

She slurped the rest of the smoothie. "Um, I love how you have all of this completely figured out."

"I do," I defended myself, cleaning the lenses of my sunglasses with my T-shirt.

"I lost a pound and a half, by the way," Mia said, changing the subject. "And I honestly feel lighter. These shorts feel looser." She pulled out the waistband to show me. "Is that possible?"

I eyed her suspiciously. "I guess?"

"Yeah, and it's like the smoothies are great. I don't even feel starving," she explained.

"How much are you spending on those drinks? Your whole paycheck?" I asked, realizing something so obvious I wasn't sure why it had taken me so long to think of it.

"Around seven dollars," she said, putting the empty cup on the floor. "Why?"

"You know we have a blender, right in this truck." I half-regretted saying it as soon as it was out of my mouth. What if the whole truck started to smell like vegan barf? It would all be my fault. "You can just make them here."

"Really?" Mia thought about that for a second. "I guess you're right! But I like the names, and how they craft the smoothie for me based on my mood. And where would I buy the ingredients? I mean, I guess I could grocery-shop. . . ."

Mia was the kind of person who needed every tiny detail figured out before she started to do anything. Sometimes she'd even schedule in our bathroom breaks at school. Like *Meet me after third period and we'll go to the bathroom on the second floor and then walk to band.*

"Oh, we could make up the names, too! That would be so much fun!" I said, and started driving to the high school, where everyone was meeting for the volunteer corps cleanup.

"You're right," Mia said. "Making up smoothie names, flavors, a fake person—we're doing it all."

She was right.

We were Katie McCormick, and we were embarking on a journey to completely humiliate Seth Manzell. We were doing this.

But then I realized this specific plan was totally stupid. "Wait a second. Scratch that. Why on earth would a snow cone truck be at the high school when school's out for the summer?" I thought out loud. "There'd be no way for the snow cone truck to know about the meeting."

"Right," Mia replied, only half paying attention.

I continued, "Plus, he's gonna want a snow cone. Seth is definitely going to want a snow cone. And then he'll see us. And then he'll know we're always in this truck. And we won't be able to drive around stalking him in it anymore."

Mia looked at me like she had realized that ten minutes ago. "Right. Also, we won't actually be inside the gym or wherever it's being held. And who knows how long they'll be in there? So basically it's pointless to go."

I thought about that for a minute. Maybe Mia's obsessive planning was a good thing for this. I was impulsive. I wasn't thinking things through.

I needed to focus and figure this out.

"We can just go straight to the beach. I mean, it's normal for people to want snow cones by the beach," I reasoned. "And then if he sees us, we can just say we're helping my uncle out for the day."

"No!" Mia whined. "We're not doing that. I changed my mind. I'm not ready to do this. I'm not ready to see him."

I picked the skin on the side of my thumb. "Unless we got Dennis to drive the truck, and we hid in the back, totally out of sight," I suggested.

"Dennis needs to be in the shop," Mia reminded me. "Plus, do we really need to drag Dennis into this? It's gonna be totally embarrassing if he finds out what we're doing."

I rolled my eyes. She was making this difficult. "Okay. Fine. You can hang in the back. I'll be the one to see him. It'll help us find out more info that way."

She hesitated a moment and then agreed.

"He didn't write Katie back, by the way," Mia told me. We had been sitting in the beach parking lot for what seemed like forever.

"That's okay," I reassured her. "He will. Give it time. Okay?"

"How come you're so sure?" she asked me. "I mean, it's not like people write to strangers online every day."

"I know," I said. "But I just have a feeling about this. She's not really a stranger. She's in the volunteer group. That's why it works!"

It was something I couldn't explain. It's not like my feeling was based on any kind of proof or evidence or anything. It was just that—a feeling. Something in my heart told me this would work.

"Well, they're not supposed to be at the beach until eleven," Mia told me. "It's only nine-thirty. Does Uncle Rick really expect us to sell snow cones in the morning?"

"I'm not sure," I said. "Maybe he just wants us to drive around. Ya know, like a mobile advertisement?"

"Maybe," Mia groaned.

"Mia." I looked into her eyes. "Just think about the moment when he realizes that we've been Katie all along. Think about that."

"There's nothing to think about yet," she said. "He didn't write back. He might never write back. That's what I'm trying to tell you."

"Fine. I know that," I admitted. "But that's the way it is with everything. You never know what's going to happen. You can't predict the future. It doesn't mean you don't try." I stopped talking and caught my breath. "We're all so passive all the time. We let stuff happen to us. We just have to deal with whatever is thrown at us. We—"

"Justine, okay." Mia interrupted me. "I get it."

"Do you, though?" I asked her.

"Sometimes I think you forget that the Seth stuff isn't happening to you," Mia said. "It's happening to me. And I get that you want to help. But it's not, like, your responsibility to fix it."

I avoided eye contact with her. I stared straight ahead through the windshield. Focused on a squirrel that was frolicking around on the grassy area next to the parking lot.

"Okay?"

I half-nodded.

"I appreciate what you're doing," she said. "I always do. But sometimes I think you're so hard on yourself because you want to solve everyone's problems. You think it's your job to make everyone feel better. But you also need to focus on making yourself feel better sometimes."

I couldn't admit that this *was* making me feel better. That taking care of Mia always made me feel better. I wasn't sure why that was. I wasn't sure what I could do to change that.

"Let's go," she said. "We'll drive around. We'll go to Bridgefield Market to get smoothie ingredients so we can make our own. And then we'll sell snow cones."

"Okay," I replied.

We'd been driving in silence for a little while when Mia said, "I can help you, too, ya know. I don't have elaborate schemes like you do. But I'm always here. I feel like you never really want to talk about what's going on with you, or your parents, or anything, I guess. But I'm here." She looked at me. "You know I'm here, right?"

"I know."

Focusing on your own problems felt pointless. They were never going to improve. And they were boring.

It was so much more interesting to focus on other people's problems.

WHEY STRONG

Whey protein, pineapple, flaxseed, beets, broccoli

JUSTINE

"OMG, he wrote us back!" Mia squealed from the back of the truck later that morning, after she'd made her first smoothie.

I had my face against the cage of our mediocre fan. It wasn't doing much to keep me cool, but it made me feel better psychologically.

"For real?" I stood up and she showed me the phone.

Yo Katie. Are you here? I'm looking for you . . .

We looked at each other like neither of us knew what to make of it.

"I'll write back," she said.

I sat down and read over her shoulder as she typed on her phone.

I bailed today. I'm a bad girl, I guess. How is it?

"Nice!" I brushed some sweat beads off my forehead with the shoulder of my T-shirt. We waited for him to respond. "I'm going to peek out again and see if I spot them."

I looked out the truck window and there were bunches of kids on the beach holding big black trash bags, picking things up, and lazily throwing them in. It was hard to see faces since we were in the parking lot and they were on the sand, all wearing matching red CT TEEN VOLUNTEER CORPS T-shirts.

Mia bit her bottom lip. "Do you see him? Why hasn't he responded yet?"

I took the phone, turned it over, and rested it on my leg. "It says he read the last message. Calm down. He's busy cleaning the beach!"

Mia laughed a little, and then we sat in silence for a few minutes, and waited for Seth to respond, and tried to stay cool.

"Let's go," I said. "We need to be at the baseball field when Little League practice lets out. That's gonna be amazing for business. Uncle Rick will be pumped when we tell him!"

"We didn't see Seth, though," Mia whined.

"But that's okay," I reassured her. "He's writing to Katie. We don't need to see him, like, ourselves."

We drove the truck over to the baseball field. I drank my iced tea and Mia sipped her smoothie. It had broccoli in it, and something called whey protein. She called it Whey Strong because her goal for the day was being strong about the whole Seth-and-Katie thing. And strong about her breakup.

Honorable goals, I figured.

When we were parked at the field, Mia groaned. "He still hasn't written back!"

"But he will."

"How are you so sure?" she asked.

"I just know."

It was too hot for long explanations; I only had energy for three- or four-word sentences.

"He figured it out," Mia said, pacing back and forth in the truck. "I just have a feeling. He knows it's us and he thinks we're complete and total freaks, and he's going to report us to the police, and everyone's going to think we're insane and we're never going to be able to go back to school."

"Mia!" I yelled. "Stop. Seriously."

She stared at me, her mouth hanging open.

"You need to stop panicking," I told her. "Just for a minute."

"I'm going for a walk," she said, and huffed away.

The only place she could walk was around the bases, and that's exactly what she did. Around and around and around. She was making me dizzy.

Finally, the teams showed up: all these miniature boys and miniature girls in too-big uniforms and too-big caps.

Business would be booming soon! I just knew it.

When Mia saw that the teams were taking the field, she came

back to the truck, covered in sweat. She ignored me, gulped her water bottle, and went to the back to make another smoothie.

So fine—this was how it was going to be.

I didn't care. It was a fact of life that friends sometimes got annoyed with each other, especially when it was three billion degrees out.

Halfway through the game, a skinny mom with giant sunglasses came to the truck window.

"What would you like?" I asked in my most pleasant customer-service-y voice.

She read the list of snow cone flavors and then sang, "Ooh, I'll have one of those," pointing to the kale, beet, coconut milk, and blueberry concoction that Mia had left on the counter behind me.

"Oh, that's, um, not for sale. My friend just made that for herself. We only sell snow cones," I said. "Sorry." I attempted to close the window.

"I'm desperate," she said, stopping me. "I didn't have time to stop at Juiceteria. And I'm stuck here for my son's game. It's nine thousand degrees out."

"Well, the snow cones are really good," I suggested. "And will totally cool you off."

"I really only do smoothies. I need my kale."

Why was it so hard for this lady to understand that we were a snow cone business? It said it right on the front of the truck.

"Well, I do have extra ingredients," Mia finally chimed in from behind me, sounding proud of herself.

I stared at the desperate lady.

I wondered if making her a smoothie would be some kind of health code violation. Or maybe it would just be an Uncle Rick violation; he really wanted an only-snow-cone business.

Mia came to the front of the truck to talk to the woman. She listed all the smoothie-making ingredients she had stored in the van refrigerator.

"Okay, all of that, and extra kale," the lady told her. "I need extra blending. Please make it as smooth as possible. I hate the chunks."

Wow. For someone so desperate, she really had a lot of demands.

"On it," Mia replied.

"You are saving my life," the lady told us, and I think she really meant it. This woman was clearly starving and dehydrated and had some kind of anxiety problem.

"It's the kale that really makes it amazing!" she yelled through the open window. "I know people say it all the time, but it's really true. Kale is honestly the most important thing to eat."

Okay, lady. We get it. Kale is great. Did she even remember she was here to watch her son's game?

"It's epic," she continued.

And right then, at the same exact second, Mia and I said *"Epic Kale,"* and burst into hysterics.

We handed the lady her smoothie. Half of it was hanging over the side of the cup, and I tried to clean it off with a napkin.

She took a sip and we stared at her. My heart pounded like we were getting graded on this.

"How is it?" I asked.

"Amazing!" she said. "Seriously. I don't know what you did. Maybe you have some kind of magic blender. This is better than Juiceteria. Way better. I'm going to tell all my friends about you."

"Wait, wait," I said. "We're really just a snow cone business."

"Oh, honey," she said, taking another sip. "That's just stupid. Make this happen."

LARGE AND IN CHARD

Blueberries, Swiss chard, carrots, wheatgrass

MIA

I remember the exact moment that I decided I loved Seth and desperately wanted him to love me back. It was a Tuesday afternoon and we were at a World Affairs Club meeting. We were going over all the rules for Model UN.

"Caucus," I'd said in a funny voice, meant only for Justine and Alexis to hear. But Seth heard too, and he turned around, and soon he was saying it. *"Caucus."*

"Let's caucus later today," he'd said, all formal-sounding.

"Oh, we'll caucus like we've never caucused before," I replied, giggling.

"Whoa, what is going on here?" Julian Glazer chimed in. "I don't think we're talking about world affairs anymore."

Seth raised his eyebrows at me, and I raised my eyebrows at him.

After that, we just started talking more and more in school, until one day he asked me to hang out. I went with him to a party at his friend Jed's house.

I was worried we'd get there and he'd stay with his boys the whole time, and I'd be left alone. But he stayed with me the whole time. Justine and Alexis didn't want to come; they didn't think they were really invited, even though I told them they were.

Everyone was in Jed's backyard playing Cornhole and hanging out. Seth and I were a team, and after we'd won a game he turned to me and said, "Come with me. You need to see Jed's basement."

I smiled, shyly, and my insides felt bubbly. It was going to happen. My hair was half up in a clip and I smelled like apple body wash. I had bangle bracelets on and they kept clinking against each other.

All the talking and laughing in school had been leading up to tonight, this moment. I was sure of it.

So Seth and I went inside, and he led me down the stairs. Jed had one of those fancy basements with a pinball machine and a wraparound couch. Big speakers, a bar, a Ping-Pong table, and a pool table. My whole house could've fit inside his basement, probably.

"It's awesome down here," I said because I couldn't think of anything else. After the words were out of my mouth, I realized how dumb it sounded. He didn't really care that much about showing me the basement.

He nodded and leaned me against the side of the pool table. He kissed me, and then I hoisted myself up so I didn't have to stand on my tiptoes. He moved in closer and put his hands on my cheeks and kissed me again. A real, true, openmouthed kiss.

I'd never kissed anyone like that before. Little kisses, sure. Middle school stuff. But this was different. This kiss made me feel like a person, like I was finally living the life I'd been waiting so long to live.

He pulled away, and I chewed my bottom lip, wondering who would talk first.

"What would you say if I said I was pro you?" He raised his eyebrows.

I laughed a little. "Um. I'd say *I'm pro you,* too."

"Good." He grabbed my hand and led me back up the stairs. We went outside and joined the group, and played another round of Cornhole.

But nothing felt the same after that kiss. The whole world looked clearer and brighter.

"I heard you make smoothies here too," a lady said, appearing at the truck window, forcing me to pause my Seth slideshow.

"Well, not really," I replied. "It was a special circumstance."

"You're clearly drinking a smoothie," the lady reminded me. "And I'd like one. I need to get on the train for Manhattan in fifteen minutes. I would like my smoothie. I'm in a hurry."

Wow. I took a step back. "Um, okay. Wh-what flavor?" I stammered.

"Something that'll make me calm, focused, relaxed, ready for the day," she lectured. "Something that'll make me feel like I have it all under control."

"I know the perfect thing." I smiled. "Excuse me a moment."

A line of customers formed behind her, and I walked to the back of the truck to start blending. Justine was standing there, perfectly still, holding her phone in midair and taking a picture of her feet.

"What are you doing?" I asked.

"My new Stan Smiths." She pointed to them. "I feel like Katie would have these and she'd totally Instagram them. But, like, ya know, in an artsy way."

"Uh, okay." I wondered if Seth would really care about someone's sneakers. Would he click *like* on that kind of photo? "We have a ton of customers."

"Smoothie or snow cone?" she asked.

"Smoothie. So far."

After a few busy mornings with lines of smoothie customers, I asked Justine if she thought we should tell Uncle Rick, or Dennis, about our side smoothie business. She said no.

I didn't really care either way, so I didn't push it.

Slowly but surely, we started to get into the swing of things. At least in terms of the business, we did. We parked the van in the parking lot by the shop every night and picked up the keys in the shop every morning.

"Wanna come with me to the bank?" Justine asked me after we dropped off the truck. She was going to deposit the snow cone money, but we were keeping our smoothie money in a shoe box in my closet. "I need to walk over from the shop. I can't parallel-park this thing downtown."

I hesitated. "Do I have to? It's so hot."

"Fine, I'll go alone," she groaned.

I was grateful for a chance to sit in the air conditioning.

Through the window, I saw Dennis swiveling around in circles on the stool by the front counter. He looked up when I came in. *"Hola,"* he said.

I smiled. "Hey."

I couldn't figure him out. I really wanted to, but I just couldn't. He was a dork, but not a dork who was trying to be a dork because it was actually dorky-cool. He was really just a plain dork, not trying to hide it at all.

I plopped down in one of the desk chairs and scrolled through Instagram, reading inspirational love quotes.

Hearts live by being wounded.
—Oscar Wilde

I clicked the little heart icon so I could go back and read this one again later.

"So how's it going, Mamma Mia?" Dennis asked.

I cracked up. "Mamma Mia? I hope not!" I looked back at my phone, hoping he'd get the hint that I wasn't in the mood to talk. I didn't want to be rude about it, but I was just too hot to converse.

"Uh, I was just saying it because, like, ya know, the Broadway show . . ." His voice trailed off. "I didn't mean, uh, that you're like a teen mom or something."

"It's okay. It's okay," I said, cutting him off, and looked up at him. His cheeks were bright red, the color of our Strawberry Sensation snow cone.

"What are you reading?" he asked. "You keep nodding to yourself."

I laughed. "Oh, just random quotes on Instagram. Like, inspirational stuff."

"You need inspiring?" he asked.

"Well . . . my boyfriend broke up with me." I rolled my eyes. "Soo . . ."

"Oh. When?"

"Like a month ago," I said. "But I'm not really over it yet. It was kind of sudden."

It sounded like I was talking about a death. But it was kind of like that. Our relationship died. And that relationship was one of the happiest parts of my whole entire life. Of course I was sad. Of course I needed cheering up.

Dennis looked away like he couldn't figure out a response. It was the perfect opportunity to stop talking, but then it felt awkward to just leave the conversation hanging in the air like that.

"I've been really into making smoothies lately," I said to change the subject. "I kind of feel like a chef now. A smoothie chef."

He laughed. "They look good."

I wondered if I should offer him a sip, but it seemed too intimate somehow. Sharing a straw. Saliva exchange. It gave me the shivers. "How's your study of losing vice-presidential candidates going?" I asked, trying not to laugh.

"I need to come up with ways to remember all of them." He

looked up, and for the first time, I realized that Dennis had blue eyes. Like, gigantic blue eyes. Maybe I was hallucinating from the heat, but his eyes were amazing. Big and dramatic. Or maybe he'd never looked at me before, or I'd never looked at him.

Something about him was relaxing, easy, comfortable. He didn't make me nervous. Everything with boys always felt so hard, like a game that I could never really win. But with Dennis, it was just, like, normal.

"Oh, um, well, that's cool. . . ." I stumbled on my words because all I could think about was Dennis's gigantic blue ocean eyes.

"Yep, if you want to quiz me, just say the word." He stood up. "I better get back to cleaning the blenders in the back. You know what they say—a clean blender is a sign of a successful business."

"They say that?" I asked.

He shook his head. "No. I don't think so."

I looked at him crooked and laughed behind my hands.

ORANGE ENERGY

Oranges, frozen banana, soy milk, Swiss chard

JUSTINE

"Can I help you?" a greeter at the door asked as I walked into the bank.

"Uh, I'm just here to deposit some money . . . for a business." I rifled through my bag. "If I can find the money . . . I may have lost it on the way here."

My scalp was sweating. I stopped my search to put my hair up in a high ponytail.

I finally looked at the guy. He was dressed in a short-sleeve plaid shirt, tucked into a pair of neatly ironed khakis. He had long, shaggy brown hair, pulled back behind his ears. It was like his whole outfit was one person and his hair was someone else.

I went back to rifling through my bag.

"You doing all right over there?" he asked.

I finally found the envelope and rolled my eyes in his direction. "Ya know, same shit, different day."

He cracked up. Like, genuine, honest laughing. "Wow," he said. "I didn't expect you to say that." He reached out to shake my hand and I reached back clumsily. I didn't shake hands very often so I wasn't sure if I had a weak handshake or a strong one.

"For the record, I don't usually dress like this." He pointed from his neck to his feet. "We gotta be business casual here. So I did the best I could." He put his hands in his pockets. "I'm Emmett."

"Justine." I smiled. "For the record, I better go deposit this money before I lose it again."

"Good plan." He nodded and guided me over to the tellers. "I'm just the door greeter, so I think I've done my job."

I smiled.

"Do you feel like you were sufficiently greeted?" He laughed.

"Oh, definitely."

Mia was sleeping over again. We were side by side on my bed staring at our phones and a tiny, tiny, tiny part of me wanted to tell her about Emmett from the bank, but I wasn't going to because there was literally nothing to tell. It was, like, a ten-second interaction.

I couldn't stop thinking about him, though. I wondered how old he was, and tried to scan my brain to see if he'd mentioned anything about his age. In the three seconds we talked on the way out, he had said something about having to retake a math final. I noted that it was kind of ironic that he was working at a bank and he'd failed math.

"Intern," he said with a shrug. "My dad's a VP, like on the corporate level. He wanted me to start here and do something for the summer. He wants me to make something of myself."

He air-quoted the last part.

Okay, so maybe we talked for more than three seconds. The important thing was that he was in high school somewhere, and that meant it would be totally legal for me to make out with him.

"Oh, post that picture from last weekend." Mia tapped my knee. "From when Katie went hiking in Glacier Hills."

"Oh, yeah." I sat up straighter. "Good call."

We made sure to keep up with Katie's Instagram and do stuff that would make her seem like a normal girl. She was living it up: communing with nature, getting ice cream at Brownies on Bond Street, shopping for flip-flops, getting manicures.

On occasion, Seth would click *like* on a photo. But he never commented.

"She never shows up at the events." Mia threw her phone across the bed after a long scroll through all of Katie's social media sites. "So Seth's not gonna get into this."

"She only bailed once, I thought." I needed to keep better track of this. Was there an app to help you keep track of the fake person you made up so you could stalk your best friend's ex-boyfriend and help her get over him? I wondered if I could find some techy person to help me make one. Genius business idea?

Maybe I was getting ahead of myself.

"I thought twice," Mia said.

I got up and walked around my room and tried to come up with a plan. "Anyway, it doesn't matter. She can't show up until the end. It's too soon. He needs to fall in love with her without seeing her in person."

"I know she can't really show up," Mia said. "But he doesn't seem to be *falling in love*."

I sighed. "Okay. We need brain food. I'm going downstairs to get us some snacks. You think about what makes Seth tick, what will get him talking."

"Bring me an apple if you have one," Mia called after me.

She was still doing the diet thing, but in all fairness, it wasn't starvation, just sensible eating. It wasn't the worst thing.

I got downstairs, and my parents were sitting on opposite ends of the couch, staring at the TV; it sounded like one of those detective shows.

I looked in, but they didn't see me.

I grabbed potato chips, Doritos, a few chocolate chip cookies, two bottles of Snapple, and an apple for Mia.

I could eat all this by myself, and I didn't even care if it was fattening. It wasn't like I was obese. Maybe I had an extra ten pounds. The pediatrician wasn't worried about it or anything. What was better—being stick-skinny like Laurel Peck or eating snacks?

I'd take the extra ten pounds and the cookies.

"I figured it out," Mia said as soon as I was back in my room with the door closed.

"You figured what out?" I licked Dorito dust off my fingers.

"We'll start talking about relationships," Mia said, biting into the apple. "Katie will confide that her boyfriend just broke up with her . . . and then we'll see what Seth says."

"You're right," I said. "Katie needs to open up . . . to reel him in!"

"Exactly!" Mia jumped up from my bed. "Let's get started!"

CAREFUL CARROT

Carrots, celery, beets, ginger, almond milk

MIA

I was so excited that Justine actually liked my idea. She never really *loved* my ideas. I mean, sometimes she pretended she did, but I could see through it.

Right then, sitting next to each other at Justine's antique desk, it just felt like things were going to go right. I couldn't put my finger on it exactly, but there was a shift in the universe.

"So what should we say?" Justine asked.

"Well, first of all, he's actually online now," I said. I showed Justine the little icon thingy that let us know he was logged in on his phone. "So we should click *like* on a recent post. It'll jog his memory . . . and maybe, just maybe he'll write us first."

She bit her bottom lip. "Ummm. You think? I guess it doesn't hurt to try."

So we clicked on his page, and he'd recently posted an article about some coach getting busted for not cracking down on a high school football team's cheating ring.

Boring. But whatever.

"We can't *like* that," Justine said. "No one likes that."

"We can make something up." I raised my eyebrows. I felt confident. Daring. I was actually in charge, in control. Katie was that way, and I wasn't. But when I was Katie—well, that's when the magic happened.

Justine raised her shoulders. "Like?"

"*My cousin goes to that school,*" I suggested.

"What if he asks who your cousin is?"

"Justine." I folded my hands on my lap and tried to be patient with her while I explained. "He doesn't know anyone at the school. He's just posting because he plays high school sports and finds the topic interesting."

"Oh. Right." She shook the crumbs from the potato chip bag into her mouth.

I typed in: *Crazy. I know someone who went to this school.*

And then we waited.

PEARFECT

Pears, honey, coconut milk, cucumbers

JUSTINE

By the time I got back from the bathroom, Katie and Seth were in a full-on back-and-forth chat.

"What's happening?" I screeched. I hadn't even been gone for that long.

Mia pointed at the computer.

I never Facebook chat with people, by the way, Seth had typed.

"Wait, scroll up," I demanded from the edge of my seat. I needed to see the rest of the conversation. I didn't realize Mia was that fast of a typer.

She scrolled back to the beginning.

Seth: Hey. Sorry I never wrote back the other day.

So it worked. Mia's plan worked. He saw Katie was online, and he wrote to her.

Katie: No problem. You're writing back now, aren't you?

Seth: ☺ I guess I am.

"There was a lull in the conversation right around here," Mia explained, pointing to the screen. "I had to say something. So I brought up the volunteer stuff."

I nodded.

Katie: So how's the volunteer stuff going? I need to show up. I don't understand why I'm this lazy.

Seth: It's summer. That's why.

Katie: Yeah, that. And I'm dealing with an f'ing breakup.

Seth: ☹

Katie: Actually, can I ask you something? Like, ya know, from a guy's perspective?

Seth: Ummmm . . . sure, I guess.

And then we were back to where we had started: Seth saying *I never Facebook chat with people, by the way. . . .*

"So, type something!" I yelled. "He's been waiting."

"That's okay," Mia said. "He can sweat it out a little bit."

I took a sip of my lemonade. "I wonder if he's actually sweating this. Does Seth sweat stuff like this?"

Mia looked at me, chewing on her pinky nail. "Um. I don't even know."

Maybe she was slowly realizing she didn't know her beloved Seth as well as she thought she did. I wondered if her heart was pounding like mine was.

"He's really into the whole dot dot dot thing," I announced.

Mia looked at the screen and said, "It's called an ellipsis."

I rolled my eyes. Of course she knew the word for it. Mia was the tippity-top of our class, and the worst part of it all was that she got As without even really having to try. "Just type. Please."

Katie: I never do either . . . it's really weird. But, anyway. Ready for my guy dilemma?
Seth: How do you even know I'm a guy? Huh? ☺
Katie: You look like a guy in your pictures, and why would you lie? That would be super creepy, you know.

Mia and I side-eyed each other. We were beyond creepy; we both knew it.

Seth: I'm just kidding. Sheesh.

"I don't know what to say now," Mia said, shaking her foot. I wasn't sure either. To be honest, I was surprised we had gotten this far. And then Seth wrote again.

Seth: Aight. Shoot. What's the dilemma? I don't have all day here, ya know.

"He seems really into this," I said, and Mia nodded. I couldn't tell how she was feeling about it all. She wasn't crying or anything; she just seemed determined. Very, very determined.

It felt like we owned Seth. Up until that moment, he'd made all the decisions—to go out with Mia and then to break up with her. But now it was our turn.

> **Katie:** So, basically, I'm really into this guy. And we were hooking up for like a month. We were having fun and everything. And then I think he got freaked out that it was becoming something more, but it really wasn't. I'm not into anything serious. I don't even want that. So he broke it off. But how can I tell him that I don't really want anything serious? Basically, I miss him, and I'm bored and it's summer. You know the deal . . .

I watched as Mia typed this, and I couldn't believe it. She was making up problems, plot lines for Katie, stuff to get Seth talking. But it was nothing too obvious. Nothing that would cause him to suspect it was us.

This wasn't the Mia I knew. Not at all. As Katie, she was confident. Katie could say whatever she wanted to say.

Or maybe it was our high school that made Mia shaky, unsure, invisible-feeling.

Seth took a while to respond. We saw the three dots that let us know he was typing but it felt like forever before his answer finally came through.

"I'm nervous," Mia said, tapping her fingers on her leg. "What if he figures it out? What if he's already figured it out?"

"Figures what out?" I asked, staring at the screen.

"That it's us. Duh."

I couldn't focus on what she was saying. All I could do was stare at the three dots on the screen and wait to see what he would say. "Oh, don't worry. He won't. Not yet, anyway."

Finally, we saw a flash on the screen.

Seth: Here's the deal: guys are dumb. They don't know what girls are thinking. If you want them to know something, you gotta spell it out.

Katie: Really?

Seth: Yup. I gotta go. Later.

And then he was gone. He signed off. We waited for a good five minutes, just sitting there, staring, not even talking to each other.

"What was that about?" Mia shrieked. "He just signed off so fast. That was weird, right?" She stood up and paced around my room.

"Calm down," I said. "He'd told us he had to go."

"I guess," Mia said, coming back to look at the computer. "I'm totally freaked out."

I put my hands on her shoulders. "Don't be freaked out. This is good. This is very, very good."

THE GUILTY PLEASURE

Mango, coconut, vanilla yogurt, peanut butter

MIA

We got to our morning spot a few days later and there was a line deep into the parking lot.

"What is happening here?" I asked Justine. "They know we don't get here until nine-thirty."

She rubbed her eyes. "Umm. I have no idea."

We opened the front window of the truck, and the line moved closer.

"Thank God you're here," one lady said. She was in a tight black tank top and yoga pants. "My class starts in ten minutes. But I need my kale!"

It was all I could do not to burst out laughing.

"We'll, uh, get started!" Justine couldn't do it—she fully cracked up.

So one by one we gave the ladies their smoothies. Most of

them ordered the same thing as the others did, every single day: our kale, blueberry, almond milk, banana concoction we started calling the Epic Kale, since it pretty much embodied our business.

A few ladies liked the mango, coconut, vanilla yogurt, and peanut butter smoothie. We called it the Guilty Pleasure. They were the chubbier moms, the ones who didn't arrive bright and early. We could count on them around noon, usually.

"My husband is so happy that I'm saving so much money," one lady said. "Compared to Juiceteria, you guys are a bargain!"

Justine and I slow-nodded at her, listening, feeling pretty proud of ourselves.

"And you two young girls, running your own business like this," she continued, rolling her lips together. "It's incredible. It really is. Feminism! Entrepreneurship!"

She was all choked up. About smoothies. About *us* making the smoothies.

The next lady came up to the counter and plopped down her oversize handbag. "I'd like one Ora—"

"What is happening here?" Uncle Rick asked, seeming to appear out of nowhere. "Everyone here for snow cones? So early in the morning?"

"Oh, actually I'd like a—" Handbag Lady tried to continue ordering, but I cut her off.

"Uncle Rick! Yes! We created this whole morning snow cone with fruit, and a tiny bit of yogurt, and it's really taken off." The lady stared at me. "So, uh, we better get back to work."

Was Justine really not hearing this? I kept turning my head to see what she was doing back there.

"I love to see you guys in action," he said. "Justine's in the back blending?"

"Yup! Come on, hop in the truck." I opened the side door for him. "Let's find her."

I held up a finger to tell the woman to wait a minute, and I mouthed *Sorry.*

"Justine!" I yelled. "Uncle Rick is here!" I hoped that would give her enough warning to put the smoothie evidence away. "Justine . . ."

"Hi, Uncle Rick!" She greeted him more excitedly than I'd ever heard her greet him before. "I'm so glad you're here, actually. . . . Can we walk for a bit? I need to talk to you about something."

Justine gave me a thumbs-up to let me know she had it all under control. They left the truck and walked around the baseball field.

We made a good team, Justine and me.

It wasn't like we were doing anything that bad, really. We used the money we made to replenish our supplies, so we weren't messing with Uncle Rick's profits or anything. . . . I wasn't sure why we couldn't tell him, but it felt like we had to keep it a secret.

He wanted only snow cones and we were going against his wishes.

I had no idea what we'd do with the money we were making. Shopping spree, maybe? Spring break trip to Turks and Caicos?

We had time to decide.

LETTUCE BE TOGETHER

Romaine, cacao, vanilla extract, kiwi

MIA

A few afternoons later, I was in the back pouring our most popular mixture into plastic cups when I heard a familiar voice.

"One Epic Kale, please," she said.

I'd know that voice anywhere.

Seth's mom.

"This is an incredible business you have going on here," she continued.

"Thanks," Justine replied. "It'll be just a moment."

Did she have any idea who she was talking to?

Justine called to me, saying she needed those six Epic Kales ASAP.

I tried to hide in the back, but I had no choice.

I had to face her.

So I brought out the tray, and when she saw me, her face lit up. It really did. I'm not just saying that.

"Mia! I didn't expect to see you here."

"Hi, Mrs. Manzell," I said.

"Oh, call me Michelle."

I smiled. It was all I could do not to crack up, because Seth and I always laughed about how his mom's name rhymed—Michelle Manzell.

"So you two are the ones behind this crazy obsession all the ladies around town are talking about?" she asked.

Justine and I looked at each other. "I guess," we said at the same time.

"This is amazing," Michelle said. She turned around. "Wow, look at this line. I better let you get back to work."

She reached into her wallet and came up a few dollars short.

"Oh, don't worry about it," I said. "You can get us next time."

"No worries. Seth's in the car." She took her phone out of her sweatshirt pocket, pushed a button, and put the phone up to her ear.

My heart pounded. I tried to make a beeline to the back, but Justine grabbed my hand and forced me to stay.

Before I knew it, Seth was right there.

Right in front of us.

"Oh. Hey." He crinkled his eyebrows and half-smiled.

"Hey." I pretended to be really busy lining up the cups of Epic Kale.

"Thanks so much, girls," Michelle said. "I'll be back, probably tomorrow!"

Seth and I stared at each other for a second.

"I didn't know you guys were doing this."

I wanted to say *Well, you knew about my summer plans and the snow cones,* but all I said was "Yeah."

"Cool." He shrugged. "I gotta run."

I watched him walk away. I kept my eyes on his back until I couldn't see him anymore.

My heart sagged, like tree branches after a rainstorm.

The freckle under his left eye. The way his hair curled on the sides. His raspy voice. His sweet lopsided smile.

He was here and then he was gone so quickly. It was like when you got the taster-size mini-cup of frozen yogurt to try a new flavor and then you really, really wanted the regular size.

We continued serving the ladies on the line. They thanked us, and asked about the ingredients, and told us how we were so "unbelievably enterprising for such a young age."

"We try," I replied, running out of responses. Every time I opened my mouth to talk about the Seth thing with Justine, it was the next lady's turn on line. And some of them had requests.

"Can you make it thick?" this one asked. "I want to really taste the vegetables."

"Hold the spinach," another lady whispered. "It gives me gas."

Wow. Too much information. Way too much information.

The line finally dissipated.

"So I guess he knows we work in this food truck now?" Justine asked before I had even brought it up.

"Obviously." I didn't mean to snap at her, but my heart was a lump of mashed potatoes. All I wanted to do was sit alone and replay that interaction over and over again in my head. I was going to add it to the Seth Memory Slideshow. "We're screwed, I guess."

"Not at all," Justine squawked.

"I don't know. . . ." I brushed some sweaty strands of hair away from my face. "Our stalking vehicle won't actually be a possibility anymore. Like, we can't stalk in it. He knows we work in this truck. Do you get what I'm saying?" I felt prickles behind my eyes.

"We weren't really driving around stalking him anymore. We're past that part. It's okay."

"Maybe." I looked down at the floor.

"We have Katie," Justine reminded me. "And that's all we need. Just remember that."

She tried to get me to feel better, and I only half-listened. Finally she went to the back of the truck to straighten up.

I took the BRIDGEFIELD ESTATES pen out of my bag and held it in my hands. It was so pathetic but it was all I had left.

"Oh, here," Justine said, coming over to me. I quickly stashed the pen away. "I found these in the back under a Post-it with your name on it." She read a flash card and handed me the stack. "Well, duh, this one's easy—Sarah Palin."

We laughed for a second.

"Why does that one even need to be on a flash card? Dennis

lived it," Justine remarked. "I don't get what this is. And why did Dennis leave them for you?"

I shrugged. "No idea."

"Let's go clean the blenders," Justine said. "We may have more customers today. We are on fire!" She shimmied back and forth and I forced a smile.

She tilted her head and stared at me. "When you leave the maze of your thoughts, let me know. Okay?"

I nodded.

Seth's half-smile from before kept appearing in my mind. And then our memories flashed one after another: the night his parents were out and we ate scrambled eggs for dinner. I sat up on the counter and watched him cook.

At the beach, when he sat behind me on the rocks and he played with my hair.

When we went to Boston for Model UN and we snuck out of our rooms in the middle of the night and hooked up behind the vending machines.

I thought he liked me. Like, really liked me. I thought he'd love me one day.

I loved *him*.

But I hated him, too.

RESET

Pineapple, chia seeds, vanilla extract, banana, ice

MIA

"I can come with you to the bank," I told Justine when we were driving over to the shop. There had been a Little League world series and a youth soccer tournament going on over the past few days, so we had lots of snow cone money to deposit.

"It's okay," she said. "Actually, can you look over the social media sites and make sure Dennis is keeping up with everything?"

It seemed like a simple enough thing for her to do, but I could certainly handle it.

"Sure."

"K, just go onto the computer in the shop and make sure everything looks normal," she instructed. "Also, can you go on as Katie on the computer and click *like* on some random stuff, maybe a status update? I feel like we've been slacking with her pages."

"That's a lot to do," I groaned, half-kidding.

She counted the money one more time before she left.

"Mia, Mia, Bo Bia, Banana-Fanna Fo Fia, Mi My Mo Mia," Dennis sang as I walked into the shop.

I giggled and sat down at the computer ready to do all of Justine's tasks. "Oh, I found the cards under the bananas in the truck."

"And?" he asked.

"I can quiz you whenever you want," I offered. "Did you leave them for me so I can learn them too?"

I checked all the Simply Snow Cones social media sites and everything looked in order. I signed on as Katie, changed her profile picture, and clicked *like* on a few things.

I sipped my newest smoothie creation: Reset. It was inspired by the Seth sighting at the truck. I needed to reset my brain, wipe away the obsessive thoughts.

I read somewhere that chia seeds help with memory and focus . . . so maybe putting them in a smoothie would help me focus on . . . other stuff. Other non-Seth stuff.

"Yeah, it'd be cool if you learned them," Dennis said. "I just like leaving them in random places for you. It's funny, right?"

"Yeah, um, I guess so." I looked at my phone to see if Seth had written to Katie. Nothing.

"It's so hard to remember it all." Dennis wheeled the desk chair around in a circle. "I should've picked something easier. Like state capitals."

I put my feet up on the desk and then took them down. "Well, that's not exciting. We learned them in fifth grade."

"Right."

"Here." I handed him my smoothie. "Chia seeds. Supposed to help with memory."

"Really?" His cheeks flushed red, but he didn't take the cup.

"Just try it."

"Interesting," he said after a sip. Then he scrunched up his nose and handed it back to me. "Come here. You have an eyelash."

I rubbed my eye.

"I got it," he said, touching the space just under my bottom eyelashes. Is there a name for that spot? "Make a wish."

I moved back a little and blew away my eyelash. "I didn't see you as the superstitious type."

"My mom taught me. She's pretty religious about it," he explained. "So, did you make a good one?"

I nodded, and we sat back down. "But if I tell you what I wished for, it won't come true."

"I know," he replied.

There was only one thing I wished for these days: for Seth to love me again.

In my mind, every penny wish in a fountain was a guarantee; every eyelash whispered away, every birthday candle blown out, every time the catch of my necklace was in the front. They would all come true.

"So . . . 1960. Anything come to mind?" Dennis asked, tapping my knee.

"Ummm." I paused. "No clue. I don't think you left me that one yet."

"Henry Cabot Lodge Jr." He rolled his lips together. "Makes

me think of maple syrup . . . soo . . . hmmm . . . a good way to remember this."

"Maple syrup?" I burst out laughing. "What are you even saying?"

He shook his head. "I have no idea. Honestly."

"You guys have the most riveting conversations," Justine said as she came into the store. I wondered how long she'd been listening. "Ready to go, Mi-Mi?"

"Chia seeds," I reminded Dennis, standing up. "Try it."

"Lovely sharing a drink with you," he called as I was out the door.

APPLE OF MY EYE

Apples, grapes, carrots, fennel, ginger

JUSTINE

"Diner tonight?" I asked Mia after work a few days later. We'd cleaned up the truck and we were just sitting on a bench on the boardwalk, relaxing.

We'd had a busy week with all the moms coming for smoothies and local day camps coming for snow cones.

"Nah," she said. "I'm prob just gonna stay in and go to bed early. I'm so tired."

"Mia . . ."

"I was just thinking about that night that Seth and I went to Coffee & Co. and you and Alexis were there. . . . Remember?"

I sighed a deep sigh. "Yeah. It was, like, two months ago."

"And we played Uno? He was so good at it." She stared out into the sea like a woman whose husband had gone off to war. "He won every time."

"Mia, I love you. You know that, right?" I turned to face her.

She nodded.

"But I can't deal with the Seth memories every day." She didn't meet my gaze, and I felt my throat prickling. "There are other things to talk about. I can't hear it all the time."

She stayed quiet, and I felt guilty. I knew she was hurting, and I knew she wanted to talk about the memories over and over again. As her best friend, I was obligated to do whatever I could to help her. But I just couldn't handle it anymore.

"I mean, it's not getting any easier with time?" I asked. "He didn't even have anything to say when he showed up at the truck."

She sniffled. "It is getting a teeny bit easier. Like, Seth used to be an elephant in my brain, taking up all my thoughts, and now he's, like, a newborn baby elephant."

I put my head back against the bench. "Okay, well, that's progress."

We needed to speed up the Katie plan. Make it happen faster. The sooner we humiliated Seth and crushed his heart, the better Mia would feel.

A few hours later, I texted Mia to see if she'd written to Seth, but she didn't respond. Maybe she really had gone to bed early.

I stared at my phone, waiting for Mia to text back. I clicked around through all my apps and scrolled through my old pictures.

And then I noticed something.

I had a new follower.

Emmett Neufeld. The guy from the bank.

I couldn't believe it. That meant he was thinking about me; I was on his mind. He had taken the time to find me; it wasn't like we had any friends in common.

I scrolled through his photos before I started following him back. It was pretty much random objects, like a really beautiful picture of a spoon, but not an antique spoon, or a family heirloom or anything. It was just a plain, old, boring spoon you'd find on the table at a diner.

It was beautiful, but I wasn't sure why.

Maybe because he took it.

MIND TRICK

Oats, cranberries, flaxseed, almond milk

MIA

"Is it weird that I'm calling you?" Dennis asked me over the phone.

"Not really. I mean, we are coworkers."

"Right, that is most certainly true. So how are you?" He guffawed. "Sorry for the rhyme."

I laughed at how bizarre he was. "I'm okay," I said. "Well, I'm not really okay."

"Huh?"

"Did I tell you Seth came by the truck the other day?" I wasn't sure why I brought Seth up to Dennis. He didn't even know him. He didn't care. But Justine was bored of it. I needed to talk about him with *someone*. "I know you're probably sick of me talking about him. I mean, Justine literally told me it's getting annoying, so . . ."

"You did tell me," Dennis said. It seemed like he was really listening, like he wasn't *that* bored. "You can talk about him all you want, but I still think that guy's a huge jerk. I don't know him. But what he did to you—that's like full-on jerk zone."

Jerk zone. That was such a Dennis expression. He was like a dad in training.

I signed on as Katie, on my computer, to see if Seth was online. "I know that. But it's like—I can't stop thinking about him."

"Just do this," Dennis said. "When you feel your mind wandering over in the Seth direction, think of something else. Like, pick a thing—something funny or random or whatever. Force yourself to think about that thing. It's a good trick. I promise."

"Okay." I was willing to give it a try. "But what should my thing be?"

"Hmmm." He was quiet for a second, thinking. "Okay, promise not to laugh?"

"Um, maybe." I laughed, I couldn't help it. "Okay, promise."

"So I have this pair of socks—I got them at Disney World a few years ago. They're covered in Mickey Mouse heads." He laughed then, so I figured I could too. "Kind of weird to have decapitated Mickeys, but that's another story. . . . They have a hole in the heel, but I can't seem to throw them away. I wear them once a week."

"And?" I asked.

"That's your thing. Think about my Mickey Mouse socks."

I pulled my knees up, wondering if something like this could actually work. "So when Seth comes into my head, think about your old, holey Mickey Mouse socks?"

"Mm-hmm."

I figured, what did I really have to lose? And it wasn't like Dennis would really know if I did it or not. "Okay. I'll try it."

"You have to really try it, though. Don't just say you're going to and then not do it."

"Okay." I smiled. It felt like this was a secret that only Dennis and I knew. His socks were a secret. And the fact that we were talking on the phone was a secret. And something about that felt exciting. "I promise."

"So my cones are selling?" Uncle Rick asked us when we were picking up the truck the next day.

We nodded.

I swallowed hard. I mean, they were selling. Just not as well as our smoothies. It wasn't a total lie.

"Really?" Even he was surprised.

I looked over at Justine; she looked as calm as could be. That was Justine, though. You never really knew how she was feeling. Nobody did. I think that's how she protected herself.

Uncle Rick kept talking. "I'm so pleased with how things are going. Dennis told me you're keeping up with ordering all the supplies and ingredients. So that makes my life so much easier."

"Happy to help," I said, moving toward the door. "We should probably get going. We always have lines of customers."

Uncle Rick looked at his watch. "At nine-thirty?"

"Well, ya know, we need to, uh, set up, and be ready." Justine jumped in quickly.

"And we told you about our breakfast snow cone, right?" I added.

"Oh. Right." Uncle Rick high-fived us. "Great work, girls."

"He has no idea," I whispered to Justine once he was out of earshot. "What's our plan, though?" I felt like I asked her this same question every other day.

"We'll tell him when we need to tell him," Justine said. "But it is kind of our thing."

We got into the truck and drove over to our usual spot by the baseball fields. We set up all the ingredients and gave the blenders a good wash.

I was in the middle of washing the kale when Justine said, "You didn't text me back last night."

I looked off into the distance, trying to appear confused. "I didn't?"

"No. You thought you did?"

I couldn't tell Justine about the Dennis phone call for a million reasons. Okay, maybe not a million, but a few really big reasons. One was that Dennis was Justine's stepcousin, so that made the whole thing weird. Also, I worried that if I told her, she'd be all like, *Mia doesn't care about Seth anymore, she got over him, finally, so we don't need to do the Katie thing.*

I mean, she was mega invested in it, and it was her idea, and she seemed so determined to make something happen.

But I always worried she'd change her mind. Get bored of it. Realize it was a pretty nutty and cruel thing to do.

I knew it was wrong. But as much as I enjoyed talking to Dennis, I still loved Seth.

I needed the Katie thing. I had to see what was going to happen.

And probably most importantly, I had to get over him.

"I fell asleep really early." I looked up at her, and her eyes were squinty and I could tell she didn't believe me. I didn't even remember she had texted. I was so focused on my conversation with Dennis.

"Really?"

"Really." I started to dry the blenders. "How was your night?"

"Fine," she said.

Did she talk as Katie on her own? I needed to know. But I also felt like I needed to pretend that Seth wasn't on my mind *all* the time.

We were quiet for a few minutes. My mind bounced back and forth between the Dennis call and wondering about any more Katie/Seth interactions.

I felt like I was getting deeper and deeper into lies I didn't even want to tell, and lies I didn't even know why I was telling.

"I *Katied it up* last night," Justine said finally.

"Is that what we're calling it now?" I asked, laughing.

"It's good, right?" She rinsed off some spinach and put it on a paper towel on the counter.

"Yeah, so what happened?" I asked her.

"He was sick. Some kind of sinus infection."

She was so skimpy with the details, making me pull this

out of her, strand by strand like spaghetti stuck at the bottom of the pot.

"Oh." My heart hurt a little bit right then. It's weird how when you're in a relationship with someone you know every little detail about their day. And then one day you're just not anymore, and you don't know the little details or the big details. It's cut off like a power outage.

"Don't look so sad." Justine cleared her throat. "He's fine."

I sat down across from her. "Just tell me everything. Please. We're in this together, right? We're both Katie. I deserve to know all the details."

She bulged out her eyes. "Okay, well, he wanted to know why girls are so, um, ya know, crazy."

I nodded, hoping she'd continue.

"He kept saying how weird it was that he was opening up to me. And maybe it was his antibiotics messing with his head. But he found me so easy to talk to. And he wasn't sure why. And then he was wondering if we'd ever meet. And why we're both so lazy about going to events and stuff."

"Interesting." I wanted her to continue but I also wanted her to stop. I was jealous. I was jealous because it seemed like Seth liked Justine. Like maybe he'd discover Katie was really Justine, and then he'd fall in love with her.

But Seth was mine.

And if I couldn't have him, I didn't want anyone else to, either. Especially not my best friend. She hated him now, after what he'd done, but what if her feelings changed one day?

Justine looked up. "That was pretty much it."

We heard a knock on the window. Our first customer. "How many Epic Kales can you make?"

"Right now?" I asked.

"Yup. My book club is having an early-morning meeting, and I'm in charge of the refreshments."

"We'll get started," Justine said.

We blended the ingredients and poured. Cup after cup after cup. And it felt great to be busy doing something.

It was nice to shut off your thoughts sometimes.

FOCUS ON THIS

Papaya, apple cider, vegan protein, cinnamon, spinach

MIA

"I think we had a break-in! An intruder!" Dennis said as soon as we showed up at the shop a few days later. "We have to tell Rick. Right away!"

"Huh?" I looked around. Everything looked intact. Nothing was broken. I'd never seen Dennis so worked up.

"Come here," he said. Justine and I followed him over to the laptop on the counter. "Look."

"Um, it's Facebook," Justine said, not looking closely at the screen. "So what?"

"Did you look at the name?" He made the font bigger. "Who is Katie McCormick and why was she in our shop?"

Dennis sat down to look closer at the profile.

Justine grabbed my hand and talked through her teeth. "Say something."

I elbowed her. "You."

"It was just logged in to her when I went to update our page," Dennis continued. "I admit, I've been lax on updating because people don't really even use Facebook anymore, but . . . who is she? And why was she in here? On our computer?" He spun around and stared at us. "Is this some kind of hack? I don't understand. I can call customer service. . . ."

"Oh, um, that's so weird," I started. "I don't get that at—"

"Dennis, calm down," Justine said, patting his shoulder awkwardly. "Katie McCormick is our friend from school. She got in major trouble and her parents won't let her use social media anymore, so she asked us to check her page."

"Really?" Dennis asked, turning around to look at the screen again. "She looks like a perfectly nice, normal girl. What did she do that was so bad?"

I glanced at Justine. She tilted her head in my direction, saying it was my turn to take over. "Oh, really crazy stuff," I said. "You don't even want to know. I actually unfriended her because my dad is, like, super strict, and he doesn't even want me hanging out with her anymore. She's going to boarding school next year. Doesn't even have a choice."

"Yeah," Justine added. "We're not even really friends. We just checked her page, as, like, one last nice thing to do before she left."

He curved his eyebrows like he wasn't totally sure what was happening, but then he signed out. "Okay, well, phew. I'm glad we haven't been robbed."

"Yeah, robbing a snow cone shop . . ." Justine laughed. "Not the smartest idea. What would the person even take?"

He shook his head. "We have a lot of money here. I don't take it to the bank every night, but I probably should. We're very popular with the over-seventy set. Go figure."

"Maybe because they all have dentures and can't chew that well?" Justine suggested. "The snow cones are soft. . . ."

"They're not that old!" I scoffed. "Maybe they're reliving their youth?"

"Maybe!" Dennis said. "Nostalgia! I didn't think of that."

"Okay, I'm going to get an iced coffee. . . . All this talk of a break-in so early in the morning has made me really tired," Justine announced. "I'll be back."

I plopped back down in my chair, exhausted too, and planned to take a three-minute power nap.

"So did you tell Justine my idea?" Dennis asked me.

"What idea?" I answered. I was so mad at myself for leaving Katie signed in. What other dumb mistakes was I about to make?

"The socks thing . . ." He wheeled his chair closer to mine so our knees touched. It got me to look up. "You told me Justine's getting sick of you talking about Seth."

"Yeah . . . I should tell her, um, about the socks."

We stayed like that, knees touching, and stared at each other for a few seconds. Like, really stared. Or more like gazed, I guess. We were just gazing into each other's eyes and it was creepy and hot all at the same time. I didn't know what was happening. Those eyes. Those gigantic ocean eyes. They sucked me in so much I had to look away.

"What are you weirdos doing?"

We jolted up and saw Justine standing in front of us.

"Having a staring contest?" She eyed me suspiciously and completely ignored Dennis.

"Yeah, exactly." I laughed. "We were bored."

"Mia." She came over to me and sat down on my lap. "You get weirder and weirder with each passing day. Do you know that?"

"I kind of had a feeling it was happening." I looked at Dennis and covered my mouth so I wouldn't crack up. "But I don't know how to stop it."

"Maybe take it easy on the kale," Justine suggested, and stood up. "I think it's going to your head or something. Come on. Ready to go?"

I grabbed my bag. "Have a great day, Dennis."

"Yes indeedy, I will."

"Yes indeedy, I will," Justine mocked him.

I elbowed her. "Hey. Leave him alone."

She rolled her eyes and walked ahead of me to the car.

Something was happening with Dennis. Little by little. I wasn't sure what it was exactly. I had no idea where it was going.

But I think that was the part I liked the best.

TRUTH OR DARE

Acai, chocolate almond milk, raw coconut sugar, raw cacao

JUSTINE

"You're crushing it," Emmett said as I walked into the bank a few days later.

"Huh?" I laughed. "What exactly am I crushing?"

"You're crushing whatever job you do. You're always here depositing money." He looked at me sideways. "Are you sure what you're doing is legal?"

"Ummmm." I glanced around. "Is this being recorded? Are you undercover?"

Then he really cracked up. There was no better feeling in the entire world than making another person laugh. It was the ultimate sense of accomplishment, of purpose, of success. It was like this small thing that didn't even really take that much effort made the world so much happier.

"Who are you?" he asked. "You're not like anyone else I've ever met. Are you some kind of immigrant from another galaxy?"

I shifted my messenger bag to the other shoulder. "You figured me out, Emmett." I started walking toward the tellers. "But I could say the same thing about you," I called back to him.

After I deposited the snow cone money, I decided to open another account, under my name, for all the smoothie money. It was too much to keep in a shoe box, and that wasn't really very safe.

We were *crushing it.* We needed to keep it separate and keep track of how much we were making.

On my way out of the bank, Emmett stopped me. "Hey, can I show you something?"

"I know about ATMs. They've been around awhile. . . ."

"Are you ever not sarcastic?" he asked me.

"I'm pretty much sarcastic all the time," I admitted. "Do you still want to show me something?"

He looked around and then grabbed my hand.

We were holding hands. Emmett and me. In the bank.

We walked silently down this long hallway, and my stomach tightened. It suddenly seemed like we were in a horror film, and I wondered if he was going to kill me or something. But there were security cameras everywhere, I reasoned, and his dad was like a senior vice-president. . . . And why would he kill me? That didn't even make sense. Unless he was some kind of psycho or something, but he really seemed normal and, like, well adjusted.

He took a key chain out of his pocket and unlocked the door.

"Oh my God," I said. "I used to come here with my mom all

the time, as a little kid. I liked it because I got to sit in those comfy chairs, and I always got lollipops. I think my mom still keeps important stuff in a safe-deposit box."

He nodded. "Cool."

Okay, so he didn't get as excited about my safe-deposit box story as I'd hoped. "So what do you want to show me?"

"Just this." He smiled and made sure the door was locked.

I gulped and looked around. There were cameras in here, too. . . .

"Um." This was definitely the stuff of horror films. I could see the headlines: *Local girl murdered in bank safe-deposit box room. Body undiscovered for two weeks. . . .* Actually, Mia would look for me pretty much right away, so it wouldn't be two weeks. "Cool."

"So when I told my friends I was working at a bank for the summer, they made fun of me nonstop, like it was the lamest job ever. They know my dad is like a super-scary bank guy, and I try to be the opposite, so they were like, *Dude. What?*"

"Okay . . ." I needed him to get to the point. I was completely and totally freaking out. We were locked in a windowless room together, and it was probably soundproof, too. My knee-pits were sweating and the air conditioning was on full blast.

"My friend Nick was like, *I dare you to make out with someone in the safe-deposit box room. . . .*"

"Are you kidding?" I gasped, stepping back from him. My skin tingled—I was horrified and excited at the same time. "I am not being part of a dare."

"How do you know I didn't already make out with Olga, the

teller who's been here since 1972?" He cracked up and drummed his fingers on his chin.

"Um, this is just getting weirder," I said, laughing too. "I don't know an Olga. . . ."

"Okay, so I didn't make out with Olga." He walked closer to me, personal-space-level close. "Here's the thing—it started out as a dare, but now I really do want to kiss you. Honestly."

"Honestly?"

He nodded. "And I know this seems really bizarre, but to be fair to my buddy Nick—I dare you to make out with me?" He lifted his shoulders.

I tried to say *yes* but no words came out, so I just shook my head up and down.

"I don't know what that means." He looked at me sideways. "Are you nodding yes to the dare? Or the really bizarre part?"

I covered my mouth, laughing. "Both, I guess." I rolled my lips together.

And then he kissed me. Just like that. Like he was a professional kisser and knew exactly what he was doing, and he didn't second-guess himself or feel nervous or insecure or anything.

Could he tell that I'd only kissed one boy in my whole life? When I was eleven, and it wasn't a make-out kind of kiss. It was only a quick peck, the kind of kiss that's over before it starts.

It probably didn't even really count as a real kiss, but it counted when you played Truth or Dare at parties in middle school. And it counted when the whole *how many guys have you kissed* conversation came up, though that came up less and less throughout high school. Because by the time you're a junior in high school, most people have moved on from kissing, and no one is keeping score anymore.

So in that sense, it kind of got easier.

But it got harder, too—because the longer you go without kissing people, and the older you get without kissing people, the more scared you get.

Like last spring when I kind of had a chance to make out with Elliott Chaffler on the Outdoor Ed trip. It was the last night and we were all around the campfire, and he was sitting next to me. We were closer than two average people at a campfire, and it's not like Elliott and I were best friends or anything.

Everyone wanted to make out with *someone* that trip; I guess he figured I would do. We were talking about boring stuff like the fact that the chem labs had gotten harder, and that everyone knew the tennis team tryouts were rigged, and then suddenly he was like, *Wanna go for a walk?*

And then I freaked out completely. I figured he'd be able to tell I'd never really kissed anyone, and our kiss would be the worst kiss in the history of people kissing, and then the whole grade would find out that I didn't know how to kiss, and I'd never kiss anyone again. So I answered, "Actually, I'm really tired," like the lamest person in the world.

I left the campfire and never came back.

Emmett pulled away finally, and I felt a little guilty that I'd spent most of our kissing session thinking how I totally ditched Elliott Chaffler.

"Let's do that again, okay?" Emmett asked.

"You have more dares to complete?"

"Maybe . . ." He half-smiled. "Just kidding. I'm just saying let's pick a place where we're not being recorded."

"What?" I shrieked.

"Don't worry." He put an arm around me. "I know how to erase the footage."

"Okay. Do it. Do it now, before we end up going viral." I picked my bag up off the floor. "I better, um, go. My friend probably thinks I've been kidnapped."

He reached over to hug me and it felt like he swallowed me up, but in a good way, like when you're bundled in a blanket on the couch and the whole world feels cozy. "I'll walk you out."

We were at the doorway of the bank when he said, "Coming back to deposit tomorrow?"

I smiled. "Hopefully."

27

LIME YOURS

Lime juice, cantaloupe, honeydew, strawberries

JUSTINE

We were seated in our favorite booth at the diner, and all I wanted to do was tell Mia about the hot make-out session in the safe-deposit box room. I was pretty sure that was illegal according to all kinds of banking rules, but honestly, no one except my mom really used safe-deposit boxes anymore.

"Ready to Katie it up?" Mia asked after she put the milk in her coffee. We had a whole plan, to really try to have a long heart-to-heart with Seth so that we could set up a time to meet him as soon as possible.

"Y-yup." I stammered a little bit.

Even though I really wanted to, I couldn't tell Mia about Emmett. She was my best friend; we didn't have secrets. But this—it felt different.

Maybe it was because she was still getting over the breakup

and I didn't want to rub it in her face. Maybe it was because once I told someone about it—once I told *Mia* about it—it would become real. What if that jinxed it?

We were signed into Messenger as Katie on my phone. We let it sit there on the table as Mia ate her fruit cup and I sipped a vanilla shake.

"He wrote to us first!" Mia yelped, and pointed at the screen. "That was the goal!"

Seth: Yo.

That two-letter word felt so significant. Yeah, it was only two letters, but it was huge.

I started to get the feeling that we were succeeding, that we were getting to the core of Seth Manzell. He was writing to us first, and it had been a few days since we'd had any contact.

Definite signs of progress.

"What should I write back?" Mia asked.

I thought about that for a second as I spooned out a lump of vanilla ice cream. We couldn't seem too overeager, like we were waiting for him. This was a game, and we were going to win.

We *had* to win.

"Just write back *hey,*" I told her.

So she did. And then it felt like seven hundred years went by while we waited.

"I have to tell you something," Mia said really fast, running all her words together.

My heart pounded. "What?"

"I talked to Dennis on the phone," she said. "The other night."

"Wait." I stared at her across the booth. "My cousin Dennis?"

"He's your stepcousin, though, right?" Mia asked, completely seriously.

"Was he scared about a break-in again?" I laughed.

"No, he wasn't scared about a break-in." She rolled her eyes. "He called me and we talked for, like, an hour, and I don't know. It was fun."

I waited for her to get to the point.

"This is so itchy now." She picked at some sunburn on her arm. She wasn't looking at me. She kept picking and picking and picking. Little specks of skin were landing on the table.

"Ew, Mia, stop." I tapped her hand. "So what did you and Dennis talk about?"

"I don't know. I mean, it was nothing. I pretty much just whined to him about Seth." She shrugged. "I need to pee."

While she was in the bathroom, Seth typed.

Seth: I've been thinking about you.

I leaned back in the booth and pulled my hair up into a bun. I had no idea what the deal was with the Dennis call, but it didn't really matter. We were Katieing it up to the fullest extent possible.

When Mia came back, I pointed to the screen. "Look at this."

"Oh my God," she said. "What? Oh my God."

"I know."

Mia grabbed the phone and typed.

Katie: Yeah?

We went back and forth like this for a while, taking turns typing.

Seth: Yeah
Katie: I'm really not that interesting . . . ☺
Seth: I think you are. You're, I dunno, mysterious.

"MYSTERIOUS?" we both yelped at the same time. And a bunch of booths around us turned to look and see what was happening.

We put our heads down.

I looked at Mia and got this eerie feeling—like little by little things were changing. Seth was still the boy who broke Mia's heart, but he was more than that now—he was our little experiment, our hobby, our revenge.

When she thought about him, what was the first thing that came into her mind? The breakup? Their memories together? Or Katie?

Katie: Honestly, I'm kind of boring, but thanks.
Seth: Are you still all worked up over that dude?
Katie: What dude?

"Genius, Justine! Act all aloof like we don't remember every single aspect of our conversations."

"Right? Right!" I was fired up. I took off my hoodie.

Seth: The one that you wanted to hook up with, or something, but he thought it was serious? Did I dream this?

I heard my phone's jingly text message sound coming from my bag, but I ignored it.

Katie: Oh yeah, whatever. I'm over him. Also, he's a counselor at sleepaway camp, so I decided it wasn't even worth dwelling on it.
Seth: Gotcha.

"That period makes it seem like the conversation is over, doesn't it?" Mia asked me, biting her thumbnail. "It looks kind of final."

"Don't read too much into it," I said. "Let's just sit tight a second."

My phone jingled again. *Emmett?* But I was determined not to let anything get in the way of this moment. It felt like things were shifting with Seth. Every day we were a little closer to him falling in love with Katie.

We stared at the screen but nothing was happening. He wasn't writing back.

We had to do something. We couldn't let that *gotcha* hang in the air like that, but we also couldn't make it look like we cared, like we were trying so hard to keep this conversation going. It seemed like so much of life was trying really hard to make it look like you weren't trying at all.

Finally, I typed:

Katie: What about you?

Mia glared at me. *"What about you?"* she screeched. "What does that even mean?"

"I'm asking him about his love life, but in a super-chill, nonchalant kind of way."

"It's also kind of confusing. I don't think he's going to get that." Mia looked around the diner like she was worried someone was overhearing this.

"Calm down, Mia," I said. "He'll figure it out."

Seth: Me?

We jumped up.

"Okay, we have an opportunity to explain," I said. "Let's keep it light. Be funny. Ya know?"

Mia nodded. "Be funny? I don't know how to be funny!"

I slapped her arm. "Yes, you do! Come on!"

She twitched her fingers a little bit as she was thinking.

Katie: Yeah, you. What's the latest on your love life? (I sound like an old lady, don't I?) ☺

"We need to work harder on not sounding like ourselves," I said. "Seth knows you talk like you're ninety-five. We can't say stuff like that."

"Oh, shit." She looked at me. "You're right."

He wasn't responding. We didn't even see the three dots to show he was typing or anything.

He knew it was us. Oh my God. Seth knew it was us.

Seth: Actually, can I ask you something? Ya know, from a girl's perspective?

We exhaled, relieved. But then I started to wonder—what if he was trying to trick us now? Like he had reversed the game and he was just playing along only to throw the whole thing in our faces when it was over.

Katie: Sure
Seth: It feels like girls are always playing games, like never really just saying how they feel . . . why is that? Like, they'll be friendly one day, and then ignore you. It's so hard to figure you people out. I don't get it.

SECOND CHANCES

Vanilla whey protein, coconut butter,
blueberries, almond milk

MIA

I wanted to run over to Seth's house right that very minute. I'd tackle him on his bed and kiss him forever and never let him go.

"Would you girls like anything else?" the waitress asked us, and we shook our heads.

"We're good, thanks." I smiled at her.

"Oh my God. He is such a girl." Justine rolled her eyes at the screen.

"What?" I ignored her comment. Thinking about stuff didn't make him a girl.

She pointed at the screen. *It's so hard to figure you people out. I don't get it.* "He is a literal girl right now."

"Stop being so rude." My cheeks were hot and all I could think about was kissing Seth. "Why is he a girl? Because he cares? That's such a stereotype. And don't we want guys to care more?"

She shrugged. "Fine, you're right. Never mind all that—he is fully into this. Like one hundred percent. You see that, right?"

"Yeah, and we need to respond," I said.

She grabbed the phone and started typing.

Katie: I don't know. I guess because guys can be such dicks sometimes. So we can't say how we really feel.

"Nice, Justine." I rolled my eyes, even though I mostly agreed with her.

"It's true," she defended herself.

Seth: Not all guys are dicks

Katie: Well, I don't know all guys . . .

Seth: True. I gotta run. My buddy just came by. Sandwich making next week?

Katie: You know it.

Seth: K, we can debate this more as we assemble the bologna . . . haha. Bologna.

Katie: Ha! Bye.

Seth: Later

"We owned that one," Justine said. "Do you see how much progress we're making?"

I nodded, replaying the conversation again and again in my head. "I still love him, though." I pushed my head back against the booth cushion.

"Mia!" Justine yelled. "Come on! He's so shady." She closed her eyes, exasperated, and stayed silent for a minute. "It's okay. We'll make it through. One day at a time."

The more we Katied it up, the more I wished I was Katie. Or Katie was me.

And that Seth was Seth.

This Seth. Online Seth. The one who opened up, and talked about stuff, and cared.

I wished it all could have been true.

CALM BEFORE THE STORM

Mangoes, peaches, vanilla yogurt

JUSTINE

"We need to tell Seth we're not coming to the event today," I said, lining up the smoothie cups on the counter. We hadn't Katied it up since the diner last Friday, but maybe that was okay. A weekend break, an absence-makes-the-heart-grow-fonder kind of thing. "Like Katie's sick, or her grandma's in town or something?"

"Totally," Mia said as she worked on the smoothie sign. It was a little silly that it'd taken us so long to make a sign. But we were busy being Katie, and making smoothies, and talking to customers, so I guess we didn't have time for aesthetics.

Mia's handwriting was the prettiest I'd ever seen. All her letters were the same size and they went in the same direction and the whole thing just looked perfect. Forget the ingredients or the names, her handwriting alone could sell smoothies.

"How does this look?"

"Amazing," I said. "Also, your arms are like super thin now. Do you know that?"

She looked at me crooked. "Huh? No way."

"Yes, they are!"

"I still have this little fat roll here." She showed me that little bit of chub between her armpit and her shoulder.

"Everyone has that, Mia." I shook my head. "Can't you just take a compliment?"

"Fine. Thanks." She shrugged.

"So what should Katie's excuse be?" I asked, wondering if I should start drinking smoothies more often too.

"Ummmm." She capped the marker and looked at me. "Grandma. People like to hear about other people's grandmas."

"They do?" I laughed.

"Totally," she said. "It's, like, a thing. Grandmas are funny. And they tell good stories, and most people can relate to having a grandma come visit."

"Okay." I reached into my pocket for my phone and saw that I had some texts.

Emmett: How's the smoothie bizzzzz? Come visit.

Emmett: Should I get a burrito for lunch? Bean or chicken?

Justine: Hi, bizz is good. Def get a chicken burrito, not even a question. I'll text u later.

"Who are you texting?" Mia asked as she stood back and admired her sign.

"Dennis wanted to know if any of our online followers had shown up, something about a ten percent discount if they tag us in a post with their snow cone. . . ." It was all I could think of on the spot.

"Oh, he could've texted me," Mia said, scratching her head.

"Yeah, true. Whatever." I read over the Emmett texts again and turned away so I could smile without Mia seeing me. "No big deal."

I opened up Messenger and started typing to Seth.

Katie: I'm not gonna make it to the event today. My grandma just showed up from Boca, surprising us. So strange. Sorry!
Seth: DUDE. You are such a flake with this. I'm gonna tell your colleges you didn't actually do the work.
Katie: You wouldn't dare . . .
Seth: True. I'm too lazy for that. But how do I even know you're a real person? Are you like some computer-generated robot my parents bought to spy on me? Why did you even join this group?

Mia sat so close to me I could feel her strawberry breath on my bare shoulder. "Ummmm," she said. "I think he's onto us. For real this time. This is freaky."

"Nah, it's okay," I said, trying to be reassuring while my stomach churned.

Seth: Can I call you? So I know you're a real girl

"Oh my God!" Mia shrieked. "What are we going to say? He can't call us. He'll recognize our voices. And our phone numbers. What can we do? We need someone to voice Katie."

I shook my foot. "Um. Okay. Let me think."

"Quick!" Mia said.

"He won't recognize my voice," I said. "Will he? I can block my phone number and call him, and if he asks why I'll say my dad's a doctor and he needs to have an unlisted number."

"You'd be calling from a landline?" Mia explained. "That doesn't even make sense."

"Shit." I stared at the phone. "Why didn't we think of this?"

"I don't know!" Mia stood up and looked out the truck window to make sure no one was nearby, listening.

Katie: Okay, that's valid. But we're going out for lunch with my grandma now. How about I call you when we get back? Okay? Give me your number.

Seth: Whatever, flake. 203-555-7883

Seth: Have fun at lunch.

Katie: Thanks. ☺

"Okay, that bought us some time," Mia said as we waited for customers. "And I have an idea."

"You do?" I asked, relieved.

She nodded. "Ya know how they have those phones to try out at the Apple store? We can call from those. They're just random numbers. Also, you can disguise your voice."

"What? No, I can't," I said. "And what if he wants to call us back?"

"I thought about that." Mia leaned on her hand. "Katie'll say she lost her phone. . . . That will buy us more time until we meet him."

The way she talked, it almost didn't even seem like she was talking about the same Seth, her Seth.

Either she had changed, or he had changed, or both of them had changed.

Or maybe it was like there were two Seths—the one Mia still loved and obsessed over, and the one who was falling in love with Katie.

Mia had them separate in her mind.

Maybe that was a good thing.

LUCKY LEMON

Lemon sorbet, pomegranate seeds, raspberries

MIA

Katie: Okay, so I'm gonna call you later, but I'm sitting here at lunch with my fam, and they're talking about stock prices or something, snooze . . . and I just realized that I always tell you about me, but you never tell me about you. What's your deal? You have a girlfriend? Does she know you talk to me? ☺

Seth: Uhhh, that's a little forward.

"Hiiiii!" Lindsay Bellson chirped, leaning on the truck counter, interrupting the Katie-and-Seth chat. "I can't believe it's taken me so long to find you guys."

"It has?" I asked, shoving my phone in my shorts pocket. "Justine's stepcousin is supposed to be posting about the snow cones all the time."

Lindsay shrugged. "I'm taking a social media break for the summer. Too stressful. Anyway, we're here for smoothies. Tell me what to get."

A second later, the rest of Lindsay's crew traipsed up to the truck. I called them the Skinnies, but they didn't know that.

Laurel Peck, Caitlin O'Leary, Anjali Mehta. We were all friends in elementary school, then sort of friends in middle school, and now . . . I wasn't even sure what to call us. People who sometimes said hi to each other, when we felt like it, probably.

"You guys, this is so amazing!" Anjali squealed. "This is, like, huge. Food trucks? Hello! You're so trendy."

Justine rolled her eyes. "Right. That's us."

"Which smoothie is going to make Mike Kim fall in love with me?" Caitlin asked. "Aren't these smoothies, like, magical? They predict the future or something . . . do you know what I'm talking about?"

"Don't, like, sue us or anything if your deepest wishes fail to come true after you drink the smoothie," Justine warned. "We're not guaranteeing anything. Got it?"

"Uh, okay, Justine," Anjali said, taking a picture of herself in front of the truck. "We're not gonna sue."

I got a nervous feeling, like Uncle Rick could see some of these posts, of people with smoothies, and then what? Did he go on Instagram? No, I didn't think so. . . . It felt like there were so many things we hadn't thought of and they were all going to come crashing down on us.

I showed the Skinnies the sign so they could pick flavors. "Who told you the smoothies were magical, anyway?"

"We heard it," Laurel said. "I forget where. . . ." She curved her finger to get me to come closer and she whispered, "What's up with you and Seth?"

My throat went lumpy. "Nothing."

"You're still, like, broken up or whatever?" Laurel cocked her head, trying to seem sympathetic.

I nodded.

"He's not hooking up with Adia anymore, by the way," she said softly. "She's hooking up with Kai Phillipe now. Little *sloot.*"

Did she really think making up a new version of the word made it sound nicer?

"Whatever. I'm kind of over it," I medium-lied. "Anyway, I recommend the Lucky Lemon. It's a bit sour, but it kind of wakes you up . . . lemon sorbet, raspberries, pomegranate seeds . . ."

"Will it bring me luck? Like for real?" Laurel asked. "I want a boyfriend for senior year. But not any boyfriend. Ya know? Someone good."

"There's someone good in our high school?" Justine mocked. "I never knew."

"Jalen Davis has gotten really hot," Laurel said. "Honestly."

"Well, it's worth a try." I smiled.

Anjali, Lindsay, Laurel, and Caitlin all ordered the Lucky Lemon.

“I’m so excited,” Caitlin said to the others, passing out the cups. “I feel like this is going to change our lives, you guys.”

Justine and I looked at each other and turned away from them, laughing to ourselves.

“Is this real life?” I asked her.

“I think so,” she said, high-fiving me.

ORANGE YOU GLAD TO SEE ME

Oranges, nectarines, coconut milk, pineapple

MIA

"You look really nice today," Dennis said a few mornings later.

Justine and I were loyal to the routine we'd developed over the past few weeks. She'd drop me at the shop, I'd make my smoothie, she'd get an iced coffee, and then we'd take the truck to the spot between the beach and the baseball fields.

"I do?" I looked down at my outfit—a black tank top and cutoffs.

"Yeah," he said. "Like more awake. Did you get more sleep last night or something?"

"I don't know, Doctor Dennis." I laughed, putting all the ingredients into the blender. I thought about how I'd weighed myself that morning, how I'd lost four pounds. It wasn't a crazy amount, but I was proud of the progress. I liked how I didn't need to lie down on my bed to get these cutoffs to zip. "How do you notice this stuff?"

He typed something on the computer. "I just do."

He looked over at me and smiled.

"Well, um, thanks." I pushed the Blend button and felt my phone vibrating in my pocket.

Alexis: You guys! Just saw Anjali's Insta of herself with your smoothie and the truck! What is happening? You guys are like famous!

I finished making the smoothie and responded to her text.

Mia: I don't even know! People like our smoothies. Text later. Miss u. xox

"Sometimes good things fall apart so better things can fall together," Dennis said, staring at the computer. "Marilyn Monroe."

"What?" I asked with my back to him, about to pour the smoothie into a cup.

"Let's just say I've also taken an interest in your inspirational love quotes," he said. "The Mobile Cones Instagram has been following a bunch of those accounts."

I poured the smoothie into a cup and some of it dripped down my hand.

"Dennis!" I screeched, and ran over to him to look at the

computer. "For real? Everyone usually makes fun of me for liking this stuff."

He nodded, all sure of himself. "I like it." He looked up at me. "Interesting perspectives."

I hugged him like it was a totally normal thing, something we did all the time. He didn't hug back; he sort of just sat there and let me hug him.

"If you're taking an interest in my losing vice-presidential candidates, I have to take an interest in your, um, interests," he said, pulling away. "As eclectic as they may be."

"Eclectic?" I laughed. "Look how many followers those accounts have! I'm not the only one."

"Okay, okay." Dennis smiled. "You're right."

Seth wasn't a baby elephant in my mind anymore.

He was merely a kangaroo.

PLUM CRAZY ABOUT YOU

Plums, peaches, yogurt, spinach, blackberries

JUSTINE

Athena Ma and all the lifeguards from the Bridgefield pool were waiting for us when we got to our spot the next morning.

"Justine, my girl!" Athena yelled, high-fiving me.

We'd known each other since nursery school, but we were never really friends-friends. She was super athletic, and I was, well, super not athletic.

"Hi," I replied. "Good morning. FYI—I'm not totally awake yet."

"Wake up! Wake up!" She put her arms over her head and started stretching. "I got my guards here, and we need to get to work, protecting the young swimmers of Bridgefield."

"So I'd suggest the Pineapple Power Plunge," Mia said, leaning on the counter. "Pineapple, cantaloupe, mango, spinach, crushed ice, protein powder, almond milk."

"You guys hear that?" Athena called back to the lifeguards;

they were all leaning on each other, looking half-asleep with sunglasses on.

"Sounds good," another lifeguard replied. I'd seen him around the pool, but I didn't know his name. He went to Oakridge High School.

The rest of them nodded. "Whatever Athena wants," Zara Sabell said. "Chase, grab one for me. I'm going back to my car."

Chase and Zara were one of the Bridgefield couples who would probably end up getting married one day, staying in Bridgefield forever, sending their kids to the schools. They were, like, counting the days until they could get a minivan and volunteer at the town firefighter parade.

"Okay, so six Pineapple Plunge whatevers," Athena said. "Thanks so much."

A few of the lifeguards went back to their cars, and Athena did jumping jacks while she waited for the smoothies.

"I need them to wake up, feel more pumped to work, ya know." She talked to us through the truck window while we made the smoothies in the back. "They're just kind of lazy."

"Uh-huh," Mia replied. "She's so hard-core," she said to me under her breath.

I nodded. "Yup."

We walked with the smoothies and handed two to each lifeguard who was still waiting.

"I heard about you and Seth," Athena said as she turned to walk away. "You're lucky you're done with him. He's scum."

Mia jolted back. We'd never heard Athena talk like this.

"Trust me. He was supposed to be on my lifeguard staff this summer, and he bailed at the last minute, something about college visits." She rolled her eyes. "BS. Total BS."

I shook my head. "I've been trying to tell her he's no good."

"Yeah. You can do much better. And you look great! Have you been working out?" Athena asked her.

"Kind of," Mia said.

Yeah, right—if walking back and forth in the truck counted as working out, and laps around the bases on the field some mornings. But whatever. She did look like she had lost weight, but not, like, too thin. Good thin.

"Thanks for the smoothies, ladies."

After Athena and the lifeguards left, we had a steady stream of customers. A day camp, some of the moms, even the staff of a local accounting office getting provisions for an "off-site." They made it sound so important.

I was at the front of the truck scrubbing the window at the end of the day. It was smudged from all the people leaning up against it, and thinking about all the sweat and germs on there thoroughly grossed me out. I decided not to think about it anymore.

I was starting to realize how good I was at controlling what I thought about and what I didn't think about. Was that a marketable skill? Maybe I could offer training sessions or motivational speeches about it. I mean, we were all hiding something. We were all trying to forget about one thing and focus on another thing. It was basically a fact of life.

"Hey, Justine."

I jumped.

Seth was standing right in front of me. Wet hair and a popped-collar green polo like he was sailing on his own yacht.

My palms started to itch. "Oh, uh, hey."

"It's Seth."

Really? He thought I didn't know who he was?

"I know who you are." I kept scrubbing.

"Oh. You seemed, like, confused." He laughed for a second, so I did too, which made the whole thing feel even more awkward.

"Here for a snow cone?" I asked, out of necessity for something to say, and hopes to speed up the interaction.

"Yeah, actually."

Was Mia not hearing this? I had no idea where she was or what she was doing.

Seth looked at his phone while I told him the flavors. "Pineapple, mango, strawberry, peach, rhubarb . . . pretty much anything, really."

"Uh." He looked up and it was obvious he hadn't heard a word I'd said. I glared at him. He was such a doofus. I'd never be able to fully understand why Mia loved him so much.

"You have blueberry?" he asked finally.

"Sure." I glanced over at his phone. He was on Messenger. With Katie! "I, um, actually, we might have run out of that. Let me, uh, go and check the ingredients."

I rushed to the back of the truck and found Mia sitting on an egg crate, chatting on her phone with Seth.

"Mia," I hissed. "Seth is here."

"What? Now?"

"Yes," I whispered. "Shhhh. What are you doing?"

She showed me the phone. He'd written to Katie again, saying he was sorry he hadn't responded about the girlfriend thing, and wondered when she was gonna call, and then he asked why she had just joined Facebook so recently.

"I got nervous," Mia whispered. "I think he's getting really suspicious. How much longer can we do this? I had to make something up. I said my parents are really strict and wouldn't let me do it until I was seventeen."

"But Katie's on every other social media thing! That doesn't even make sense," I whispered back. "No one in the world would ever believe that. Why didn't you discuss with me first?"

"She joined them all at the same time," she hissed. "He's really here? Right now?"

"Yes! He's at the window . . . chatting with YOU!" I clenched my teeth and made the snow cone. "Just stay here."

"Hi, sorry," I said when I got back to the front of the truck. "Here ya go." I handed him his snow cone.

He looked at his phone for a second and then back up at me. "Uh, how much is it?"

"Three dollars."

"Really? You can charge way more than that, ya know?"

I glared at him. "Thanks for telling me how to run my uncle's business."

He laughed. "Um, okay, sorry." He looked at me and then muttered under his breath, "You haven't changed."

"I know I haven't. It's been less than two months since school ended. People don't change that fast." I glared at him. "In fact, I don't think people change at all."

He hesitated for a second. "Yeah, I guess you're right. It feels like longer since school let out, though. Doesn't it?"

Was he really just standing there and continuing this conversation with me? Like he wanted to stay and talk? I didn't get it.

"I guess," I said. "I need to get back to work."

Seth walked away, hesitated, and then turned around. "See ya, Justine." He paused and slurped up some of his snow cone. "Tell Mia I say hey."

"Why should I?" I asked. He'd broken my best friend's heart, and he was just living life like a normal person, like nothing had even happened. He was just ordering snow cones and wearing popped-collar shirts like he'd done nothing wrong!

"I dunno," he said, walking away and not looking back at me this time. "It's just, like, a thing people say . . . whatever."

"So what happened?" Mia asked me as soon as he was gone.

"Didn't you hear?" I asked her, cleaning the counter.

"Yeah, well, I heard him tell you to tell me to say *hey*."

"That was basically it," I mumbled. I didn't want to tell her anything more. She didn't need to endure any more of the Seth Show. Who did he think he was, just showing up at our business like that? "Let's just finish cleaning, okay? I'm really tired."

We cleaned quietly, not really talking, and I wondered if Mia was all mushy again after the Seth interaction. Was she going to take out the pen and sit by herself staring at it for the rest of the night? I looked for any signs of her emotions.

Nothing was clear, though. She was just cleaning—spritzing the counter and putting ingredients into sealed containers, making sure the covers of the sorbets and yogurts were all on tight. The usual end-of-day stuff.

"I don't feel like stabbing myself right now," she said after we were done. "That's kind of a big deal."

"What do you mean, you don't feel like stabbing yourself?" I asked, starting to drive back to the shop.

"I mean, he's not even a newborn elephant in my brain anymore. He's not even a kangaroo. He's, like, a standard poodle now? Maybe I'm getting over him," she said. "Like, little by little. We're doing great with the smoothies, and people are noticing I've lost weight, and I feel pretty okay. And I mean, I'm not freaking out right now."

"That's good," I said, trying to focus on driving. I wasn't sure if I should believe her. "But I don't think I can make the Katie call now. My voice may sound too familiar to him."

"You think? Maybe Katie's already lost her phone?" Mia suggested.

"Does Katie have a landline?" I asked her.

There were so many things we hadn't thought about, and I was mad at myself for not focusing on the details. But we were so close to victory; we had to work with what we had.

POSITIVITY

Pumpkin seeds, strawberries, raspberries, peach sorbet, kale

MIA

"Mia. 1908. Go," Dennis said a few mornings later.

"Oh, for real? This is still going on?" Justine groaned.

"I know this one!" I yelled. "John Kern. *JK. 1908.* That's how I remembered it!" I bowed, waiting for them to share in the excitement. "Isn't that great?"

"Amazing!" Dennis clapped and then wrapped his arms around me. A real hug. Not like he was just staying still, being hugged.

It lasted for a second, and then he pulled away and rubbed his palms on the sides of his pants. "Uh, okay, I got a little excited there."

"Okay. Wow." Justine laughed. "I have no idea what's going on. But losing political candidates aren't usually this exciting. And we have smoothies, I mean snow cones, to make!"

Justine walked in front of me and I turned around to say goodbye to Dennis. *Call me later,* I mouthed.

❤ ❤ ❤

"We have a line of customers and Seth is writing to Katie," Justine said when we were in the back of the truck getting the ingredients ready.

"Already?" I asked.

"See for yourself." Justine handed me the phone.

Seth: You still haven't called . . .

Katie: OMG. I am so sorry. My grandma just left, and I lost my phone when we went into the city the other day. My parents are so pissed bc I've lost like 3 phones, so I'm banned from using the landline, and I can't get a new phone for a few weeks.

Seth: That sucks. How are you messaging me now?

"Crap. How am I typing to him?" I asked Justine.

"An iPad," she said. "Now, come on, we need to serve these customers. I never thought I'd say this, but we gotta stop with Katie now."

Katie: iPad. Ugh. And now I gotta go help my mom bring in the groceries. Another punishment. NEVER LOSE YOUR PHONE.

Seth: Later.

"Wait, who's in line?" I asked Justine as she walked to the front of the truck. "Anyone we know?"

She looked around. "Yeah, actually. It's like the whole Mathletes team. They wake up early. In the summer. Kind of sad."

"We wake up early. In the summer," I reminded her, walking to the front of the truck.

"Mia, this is so incredible!" Rita Mellsen, cocaptain of Mathletes, said. She was always trying to get me to join, but competitive stuff just wasn't my thing.

"Thanks. You guys are, like, all hanging out, this early in the morning? Is this a team meeting or something?" I asked her.

Rita pushed her sunglasses to the top of her head. "It is, actually. And we need to step up our game." She paused. "Our math game. We have some steep competition this year—hello, East Oakridge—and we need to crush them!"

"Okay . . . Go, Wildcats!" Justine twirled her fingers in the air. "Rita, tell us how we can help."

I cracked up and then bit my cheek to stop myself.

Then Jamal Curtis, the other cocaptain, chimed in, "We need a brain-food smoothie to help with concentration. Blueberries, avocados, dark chocolate, some leafy green veggie. I've researched it."

"Brain food," Justine and I repeated at the same time.

"I'm on it," I said.

"Great," Rita replied. "We'll take eight of them."

"The smoothies are coming, guys!" Jamal yelled back to the team. "Get ready. We are going to decimate the competition."

After the Mathletes left, Justine and I sat down for a few minutes to take a break. "I think Dennis is really rocking the social media. People are hearing about us. Ya know?"

"Yeah," Justine said. "Mathletes, moms, lifeguards, the Skinnies . . . everyone loves our product."

"I'm too tired to move," I said, lifting my foot. "Foot five?"

Justine lifted her foot too and we touched flip-flops. "Foot five."

Seth: Well, since you're never gonna call me and you're never gonna show . . .

"Um, what does this mean?" I showed Justine the phone.

She jolted up and read it over. She started to type.

Katie: I know, I'm honestly a huge flake. You should know that about me. But I'm a good person. And I'm cute. ☺

"I felt like I had to step up the flirting, offer something new," she explained. "He was obviously thinking about Katie."

Seth: You are cute . . .

"Give me the phone," I said. "I have a good response."

Katie: Well, you never answered my question. Do you have a girlfriend or not? How do I know if it's worth it to show up, call you, get to know you? You may be taken . . .

I finished typing and chewed my cheek, waiting for him to respond.

At first I'd thought it was Katie who gave me the confidence, the ability to say things I'd never say in real life. I was hiding behind a fake person and a screen, and everything was fair game.

But I was starting to realize that was only part of it. I felt good as myself, too. More brave, more self-assured.

Maybe Katie was the gateway, but Mia was beginning to take over.

Seth: Oh so that's why you're avoiding me?

Katie: Answer the question, dude.

Seth: I'm flying solo these days.

My heart pounded. "So he's single?"

"We knew Adia moved on to Kai," Justine reminded me.

"Yeah, but Seth could've moved on to someone else too," I said as I typed.

Katie: Well, that's good to know . . . ☺

Seth: Not so great, actually. I broke up with this girl, and then hooked up with someone else, and then she ended that, and now it's like major dry spell.

Justine made a face like she was sickened. "Ew, the way he said that, or typed it, made it sound gross and unappealing. Like girls were conquests and nothing really meant anything to him."

It was true, but he was talking about me! I had to dig further.

Katie: Sorry to hear that. Why'd you break up with the first girl?

"We are getting the insider info you've wanted!" Justine yelled. "We are crushing this!"

"I'm freaking out." I stared at the phone, waiting for his response.

Seth: This other girl wanted to hook up with me, and I dunno, I wanted to hook up with her, too. We were at this party, and she was, like, all over me and . . . ya know . . .

I started breathing heavy angry breaths. I clenched my teeth together. I wanted to shoot daggers out of my eyes through the phone. Directly at Seth.

Katie: So basically you're like every other guy on the planet?

Seth: Huh? What's that supposed to mean?

"I'm tempted to come clean," I said. "Tell him it's us. I'm so mad at him right now."

"I'm glad you're mad, but we can't come clean yet," Justine said, tapping my knee. "It wouldn't have the same effect. We need to ruin him. We're almost there."

Katie: Haha, nothing. I'm just kidding. Listen, I gotta run. Look at my picture in the meantime. ☺ I'm worth waiting for, I promise.

"This is bad," I said. "I mean, he's bad, he's terrible, he's fingernail dirt. But we're, like, not so great. . . ."

Justine reached over for a sip of my smoothie. "We're not so great. I know. We're doing a kind of bad thing to a very bad person. It's not even in the same bad category."

"So?" I asked.

"So, we're doing it for a reason." She nodded, all reassuring. "And we'll never do it again."

NUTS ABOUT YOU

Almond milk, peanut butter,
chocolate powder, vanilla yogurt

JUSTINE

"What are you doing here?" I asked Emmett.

No one ever showed up at my house unannounced, so my heart was racing when I heard the doorbell and saw him standing there. My first thought was that it was bad news—I'd done something wrong with the money, or someone had seen the footage of us in the safe-deposit box room and he was fired and never coming back.

"I wanted to surprise you," he said. "Remember the other day when I asked where you live because I was trying to get a sense of the town?"

I left the door open and went outside to stand with him on the front steps. I looked back to make sure my parents weren't listening. "So . . . you're stalking me?" I tapped my fingers against my lips.

"Well," he said. "I don't know if I'd call it stalking . . . I just wanted to see you again."

I smiled. So it wasn't bad news; it was good news, actually. I breathed in, trying to get my heart to calm down.

"Justine," my mom called to me. "Who's here? Close the door. You're letting out all the AC!"

"Sorry, Mom. Just a friend. We're going for a quick walk around the block. Be back soon." I ran my words together as quickly as possible.

"What? Who? Justine, come here and talk to me." I closed the door. Hopefully she'd be asleep by the time I got back.

"Your mom sounded a little freaked," Emmett said as we walked.

"She's always freaked," I said. "Don't worry about it."

"My mom gets like that too," he admitted.

"Really?"

"Yeah, my parents got divorced a few years ago, and it's, like, she hasn't totally figured life out yet," he said, and was quiet for a minute. "I don't know why I'm telling you all this."

"It's okay, I feel like my parents are always on the verge of divorce," I replied. "I never tell anyone that, so consider yourself lucky."

"Considered lucky." He saluted.

We walked for a little while longer and then sat down on a bench at the edge of our neighborhood park. The playground was empty at this time of night, and the swings moved back and forth in the breeze. The air had that sticky summer thickness; it smelled like grass right after a rainstorm.

My phone twinkled, and I saw the little Messenger bubble pop up.

Seth: Yo. Hope I didn't scare you off earlier

My heart thudded. I had my own life to focus on, but I had to handle Katie's life, too. I quickly shoved the phone into my bag.

"Your boyfriend texting you?" Emmett asked me.

"Boyfriend? What?" I scratched my cheek. "No, no. It was nothing."

"I just want you to know, I don't kiss every girl who comes into the bank," Emmett said. "That would be gross."

"Yeah . . ." I played with the frayed ends of my jean shorts. "There are a lot of really old ladies in this town. And Olga."

I loved how Olga the teller had become our private joke. She was actually a really nice lady who knew everything about banking and could probably be the CEO of a major corporation if she wanted to.

He laughed and leaned back. He put his arm around my shoulder. "Did you come here all the time as a kid?"

I nodded. "Yeah, all the time, like every day."

"For real?" he asked. "I honestly never know when you're serious."

"I'm being serious," I said. "Why would I joke about that?"

"No idea."

I draped my leg over his knees. "Are you enjoying your time in this delightful town?" I asked. "That was sarcasm, by the way."

He laughed. "I got that. Um, it's okay. I kind of miss Boston, but this is cool for the summer." He paused. "And I met you, so that makes it better."

"I know. I'm a treasure."

"See? What kind of response is that?" He moved away from me a little bit, and my foot dropped to the ground.

"What?"

"Nothin'," he said. "You *are* a treasure."

"See!" I hit his leg. "Now I don't know if you're being serious!"

He moved closer to me again, and put his hand on the back of my neck, and pulled me toward him. He turned his head, and then his lips were on my lips, and his arm was on my back. We were close, wrapped up together like those pretzels you get at the airport. He smelled like fresh-scent deodorant and hair gel.

My phone twinkled in my bag again, but I ignored it.

HONEYDEW YOU LOVE ME?

Honeydew, lychee, almond milk, protein powder

MIA

I had no idea what Justine was doing. She wasn't responding to texts. And Katie kept getting all these messages from Seth. I had no choice but to Katie it up by myself. I knew I could handle it.

> **Katie:** You didn't scare me off. I know how guys are. I'm not one of those girls who like expects every boyfriend to be all emotional and stuff. UGH. My mom is bugging me to do something. AGAIN. BRB.
>
> **Seth:** Moms seem to do a lot of that, don't they? Are you ever getting your phone back?

I waited a few minutes to make it seem like I was actually doing something, and then I responded.

Katie: I have no idea. I have to earn it. Whatever that means. I mean, they didn't let me go on social media until I turned seventeen . . . so you get the idea. So what's up with you?

Seth: Nothing. Going out in a few. What about you?

I needed to fire up this conversation.

Katie: Actually, I did something I shouldn't have done, and I'm all messed up about it . . . and I want to call you, but I can't . . .

Seth: What'd you do?

Katie: I rekindled with an ex-boyfriend, but, like, I'm sure it meant nothing, but I kind of want to do it again, but my friends don't think I should, and I don't know . . .

I couldn't stop with the ellipses. It was just so satisfying. It showed that there was more to come. And I guess there was always more to come.

It was like a sense of hope in punctuation form.

Seth: Rekindled? That's kind of a funny way of putting it.

Katie: I guess I was trying to say we hooked up, but in a more graceful way.

Seth: No need to be graceful with me. Anyway, who cares what your friends think? Do what you want to do.

Katie: Ok. But I don't even know what I want!

Seth: Well, that's where I come in . . .

What did that even mean? That he knew Katie wanted him, or that he'd help Katie figure out what she wanted?

Seth: Too bad you don't care about helping the people of CT like I do? Hee hee.

His *hee hee* annoyed me.

Katie: I do care . . . but . . . I'll come soon. I promise!

Seth: Ok, ok. I'll believe you. Listen, I gotta run. Don't overthink the hooking up, rekindling thing. It happened. It's done. That's it. Girls always overthink everything. Later.

And then he was gone. Where was he going?

I heard my phone buzz from where it was charging across the room.

"Hey, Mia," Dennis said after I answered. He was out of breath, like he was walking and talking.

"What's up?"

"You okay? You sound upset or something."

I curled onto my side, on my bed. I didn't really feel like talking. I'd stay on the phone five minutes, tops, and then hang up.

"I'm fine," I said. "Just tired." That was always my default, something to say when I couldn't think of anything else. I wondered if everyone had a default response, or if it was only me.

"I'm just gonna come right out and say this," Dennis started, and I wanted to cut him off because I was scared of what he was going to say. But I didn't. "I know we talk on the phone and stuff, but I want to hang out with you, outside of work. Can we schedule some time to do that?"

Schedule some time? I laughed even though I hadn't meant to and it was probably rude.

"Why are you laughing?" he asked.

"I don't even kn—" I couldn't get the words out, I was laughing so hard.

"Your laugh makes me laugh!" he said, cracking up too.

"So can we?" he asked when we finally caught our breath.

"We can hang out," I said. He was actually asking me to hang out. Another boy was asking me to hang out. Someone other than Seth. Someone funny, and interesting, and unique even though he didn't try to be any of those things.

"Okay," he replied. "My parents—uh, I mean my mother and Rick are going out of town next week . . . so . . ." His voice trailed off and I was pretty sure I knew what he was saying. It was pretty bold for Dennis. I wasn't one hundred percent sure he'd ever even kissed a girl. ". . . you can come over. We have a hot tub."

"Okay, sounds good," I said. "We can hang out when they're home, too, ya know." I wasn't sure why I said the last part. It made me sound kind of lame. But I didn't want him to think he had to hide me or anything.

"Yes, um, of course." He paused and it felt like three years went by before he said anything else. "Listen, Mia, I'm new at this. I have no idea what I'm doing when it comes to girls. I didn't think you'd be into the losing-vice-presidential-candidates thing, but you sort of are, right? I mean, I really don't know."

His honesty was kind of shocking, since people are always pretending to be more experienced than they are, cooler, smarter, pretty much more anything than they are.

I guess when you broke it down—people were always pretending. Did we ever know anyone's real self?

"Don't worry," I said, reassured and relieved from everything he was saying. "I just think it's a cool, random thing you're trying to learn, so yeah . . ." He was quiet then, so I added, "And you should know, I'm not, like, the most experienced girl in the world, either."

"Okay, well, um, thanks for telling me. I'll see you tomorrow," he said. "'Night, Mia."

"'Night."

I put down the phone and I felt like one of those sappy girls who claim they *can't stop smiling.*

But I actually couldn't stop smiling.

Dennis was *Dennis.*

And maybe he didn't know that he should pretend to be anything else, or maybe he just didn't even care to try pretending.

Or maybe he didn't want to pretend.

Maybe he was okay being himself.

PUMPKIN PARADISE

Pumpkin seeds, coconut, banana, honey, yogurt

MIA

"Hey," Seth said, out of breath like he'd run three miles to get to the truck. "I'm back again for a snow cone. And a smoothie. My mom is obsessed with your smoothies."

I tried to think of the wittiest thing possible to say back. "Well, they are amazing" was the best I could come up with.

He nodded. "So . . . one blueberry snow cone, and one, uh, Pumpkin Paradise, please?"

"You don't sound so confident in your choice. Sure that's what she wants?"

He half-smiled. "I'm sure."

I handed him the smoothie, careful that there weren't drips down the side of the cup. "Hope Michelle Manzell enjoys it."

After I said it, I worried he wouldn't remember our joke.

He shook his head. "What a name. What a name."

I smiled.

It felt like there should have been more to add, but nothing came to me. There wasn't a single thing in the world to say at that moment. My mind was blank. And he was silent too.

He took a big bite out of his snow cone. "So, okay, uh, see ya around."

After I was sure he was out of earshot, I turned to Justine and asked, "Why do you think he came by?"

Justine looked at me sideways, leaning on the counter. "He was getting a smoothie for his mom. And he wanted a snow cone."

"I know, but it's a little weird, right?" I asked her, forcing conversation, trying to figure out why she was so quiet. "She could get them herself."

"He's weird, Mia," she said, bulging her eyes at me. "I've been trying to tell you that. Forever. What about Seth has ever led you to believe that he's anything but weird? And I don't mean weird in a good way. He should be scared to see you after what he did. But he just sails through life like it's all owed to him."

"Yeah, well, that's true."

"And he's, like, fully flirty and opening up to a person he doesn't know, and has never met, and who never even shows up," Justine reminded me, raising her eyebrows. "At all."

"Right. . . ." A tiny corner of my heart started to feel guilty again. I wanted to hurt him and humiliate him and make him feel the pain I'd felt. But maybe this was too much.

"I mean, part of this experiment is to get you to see how creepy he is," she said. "You're not seeing that . . . are you?"

"I am," I defended myself. "I definitely am."

"Good," she said. "Then my plan is working."

"Can we be arrested for this?" I asked her, sipping a smoothie. "I'm getting a bad feeling about it again."

She shook her head. "I don't think we can get arrested." She folded her arms across her chest. "Plus, we're minors so it's, like, can we really get in trouble? Anyway, we'll stop it before it gets dangerous."

"D-dangerous?" I stammered.

"Don't worry, Mi." She put a sweaty hand on my shoulder. "Just trust me. I got this."

I tried to trust Justine, but something inside me felt twitchy. What he had done was terrible, but maybe I didn't need to be terrible too.

Maybe I could just live my life and be okay. The whole *the best revenge is success* thing.

I mean, we were successful with the smoothies. And that was great. And Dennis liked me. And I liked him. And the hot tub sounded exciting.

I was okay on my own, without Katie. Katie was simply a crutch I needed until I felt good again.

And maybe I was feeling good now. I mean, my heart hadn't melted when he walked out to his car before. And after he was gone, I hadn't felt the need to run away to be alone. I hadn't played the interaction over and over again in my head like a YouTube video.

There was progress happening here. Definite progress.

BRAVOCADO

Avocado, strawberries, vanilla yogurt, ice

JUSTINE

It was early August and I still wasn't one hundred percent confident that we'd be able to make this Seth-and-Katie meetup happen. We had to get it done with some time to spare before school started in case something really crazy and embarrassing happened.

I knew we were close, but I still worried that it would all unravel and end up as nothing. I told myself I was confident it was going to work, and I told Mia I was sure of it.

I reassured both of us that it was okay and totally acceptable that we were doing this. He had hurt Mia. She was suffering in a major way. And that meant we had to get back at Seth, make him suffer.

But the truth was—I was lying to both of us. About all of it.

I was also lying that I felt okay about keeping all the money hidden from Uncle Rick. I felt terrible about it, and we didn't have a good plan for what to do with the money.

But it was technically our money. We'd made it fairly, and we paid for all our own supplies, from the money we'd made.

So there was really nothing wrong with it.

"Hey," Emmett said, coming out of the bank during his break. "Have you been waiting awhile?"

"Nah," I said.

"Wanna walk?" He put on his sunglasses.

I had chocolate graham crackers in my pocket, and I could feel them melting. Normally, I would have ignored them, afraid to eat in front of a boy. I'd let them melt all over the place, into my sweatshirt pocket, and then I'd throw away this hoodie when I admitted defeat, that it would never come clean.

But with Emmett, I felt like I could take them out, ask him if he wanted one.

He knew I wasn't the skinniest girl in the world, but he liked me anyway. Maybe stick-skinny girls weren't his thing. "Want a chocolate-covered graham cracker?" I asked him.

"How fancy."

I handed it to him. "Sorry it's a little melty."

"Melty is okay with me," he said. He licked his fingers when he finished it, and then grabbed my hand. That would probably seem gross to most people, but I didn't mind.

"How's the bank today?" I asked him as we walked.

"Lame," he said. "I'm waiting for something to really grab me. Like in life. Ya know?"

"Yeah, I know what you mean."

"But you're, like, into that food truck thing you got going on, no?" He looked at me, and I looked at him, and it seemed like all the air in the entire world had been sucked away through a teeny, tiny cocktail straw.

It felt like I was the only person on the planet he wanted to talk to. There were no distractions. There was nothing else on his mind.

I wanted to bottle that look, that smile, and keep it on a shelf in my room so that I could take it out whenever I felt sad, or lonely, or invisible.

"Yeah." I stared at the grass and swallowed hard. "I like it."

"Let's sit," he said.

We sat down in the half-mud, half-grass area, but I didn't worry about getting my shorts dirty. We were in this secluded part of the park and the whole world was a million miles away.

He leaned back on his arms. "I found this spot when I was hiking a few weeks ago. Look up."

The trees above us were all intersecting, like they were planned to go that way, like someone had followed a pattern and made them into this beautiful tapestry.

"Pretty awesome," I said.

"Right? Don't you think the blue of the sky and the green of the trees just, like, look good together? I'd wear a striped shirt with those exact colors, ya know?"

I nodded. "They do look good together. Like it was part of a whole elaborate plan for the world."

"Exactly." Emmett took out a bag of pistachio nuts and started eating them, placing the shells in a neat pile. He didn't say anything forever and ever after that, and I didn't either. We just sat there, and every few seconds he'd offer me a pistachio. Sometimes I'd take one, and sometimes I wouldn't.

I liked that Emmett thought about stuff like this, and noticed stuff like this, and wasn't embarrassed to admit it and bring it up.

I reached into my bag to find my phone and take a picture. Katie would love this; I had to post it for her.

We sat there for a while, staring at the trees and the sky and crunching pistachio nuts. I wasn't sure I'd ever had a time like this before—where I felt so completely safe and comfortable with someone. Maybe because summer was ending soon, and Emmett would be leaving, and I'd never get to see him again. And also, he didn't know anyone I knew, and I didn't know anyone he knew.

In a sense, we were both anonymous to each other.

We weren't that much different from Seth and Katie, even though we were hanging out in person and not chatting online.

I wanted to tell Mia all about him.

But more than that, I wanted Emmett to be mine, and mine alone. Just for a little while longer.

RAINY-DAY RESPITE

Strawberry, banana, mango, plain yogurt

MIA

It rained for a week straight. Justine was antsy. Business was slower than usual. The moms still came for the smoothies but that was pretty much it. No Little Leaguers coming for snow cones. Maybe the Skinnies were away? The Mathletes were at a competition in Florida. I figured the lifeguards had the week off and were all busy working out.

I wrote my name over and over again in the condensation on the truck window.

Seth: I'm going away, to London for a few days. My parents refuse to pay for overseas data. They want some quality family time. Blah blah blah.
Katie: That sucks. I know it sounds weird, but I'll miss you.

Seth: I know what u mean. I keep fantasizing about us meeting . . .

Katie: Me too . . . So when you're back?

Seth: It's gonna be so hot . . . we don't know each other, but we also really know each other. You know what I mean?

Katie: Totally, but what if you forget all about me when you're away?

Seth: It's possible. I mean, British girls are pretty hot, too.

Katie: ☹

Seth: Just kidding.

"OMG, we are killing it," Justine said when I showed her the phone. "I mean, you're killing it. You're doing a ton of the work."

"I'm getting kind of good at it, right?"

I was proud of myself for all the Katie conversations, but the Dennis hangout was occupying a corner of my brain too. I was half-upset that Seth was leaving the country and half-excited for the hot tub with Dennis.

Justine nodded, slurping the rest of the strawberry-banana-mango-yogurt smoothie she'd made. The Rainy-Day Respite. "Yeah, you're, like, amazing at it. What are you doing tonight?"

"I gotta hang with my dad," I lied. "He wants to start watching some Netflix show together."

"Really?" She looked up, getting the last bits of smoothie from the bottom of her straw. "That's sweet."

I had to make *something* up. Alexis was still in the Catskills and

I didn't really hang out with anyone else. I contemplated saying that Laurel Peck and the Skinnies had invited me to see a movie with them, but they hadn't shown up lately so it didn't seem believable. And even if she did believe me, what if Justine wanted to come too? Too risky.

"I think he's just realizing that I'll be going to college soon, and then he'll be alone, so he's trying to make sure we spend time together," I explained. I wasn't sure when I'd become so good at lying.

"Nice," Justine said. She got up to throw away her smoothie cup. "This is the slowest day ever. Should we just close early? Go home?"

"It could clear up," I said. "Let's just stay here."

We couldn't leave yet because Dennis and I had this whole plan that we'd go back to his house when Justine went to the bank. If I went home, he'd have to pick me up. I'd have to tell my dad about him. It would make things more awkward.

"I need to go to the bank again, actually," Justine said. "There's something weird with our smoothie account. I want to make sure we're the only ones who can access it. I think it got linked with the business account somehow."

"Really?" My throat got itchy. "Maybe keeping the money in a shoe box was a better idea?"

"Don't look so nervous," she told me. "I just need to make sure we sign this one form."

I wasn't totally sure what she was saying made any sense, but I knew Justine wouldn't want to get us in trouble.

"So I'm gonna go," she said. "I can drop you home if you want? Or . . ."

"I can come with you to the bank," I said.

"Nah, it's okay, I feel like it'll take a while, with this form, and it'll look more professional if I go alone." She cracked her knuckles. "It's not a big deal but we can't look, like, immature and stuff. Ya know?"

I wasn't really sure what she was talking about, but I couldn't focus on it. My mind was on my plan with Dennis. I had no idea what was going to happen.

"Do you mind dropping me at the shop, actually?" I asked. "I don't feel like going home yet."

We went inside and Dennis was on the computer.

"Oh, hey." He looked up. He started to get twitchy when he saw Justine there, but I shook my head a little, trying to say there was no reason to worry.

"Hey, slow day," I explained. "I'm just gonna hang here for a bit. Do you mind?"

"Hmm . . ." He stared at the screen, only half paying attention. *"'Tis better to have loved and lost than never to have loved at all!"*

"What is he talking about?" Justine looked at me.

"Beautiful quote, right, Mia?" Dennis asked. I covered my mouth with my hand to hold back the laughter.

Justine walked over to look at the computer. "What is happening? You've gotten Dennis into your quotes now too?"

Dennis put his hands behind his head. *"Love does not consist of gazing at each other, but in looking outward together in the same direction.* Antoine de Saint-Exupéry."

"Okay, Dennis." Justine smirked. "Don't try too hard."

When we heard the door close, I sat down on a rolling chair and inched closer and closer to Dennis, until the sides of our chairs were touching and I could smell his pine-scented shampoo.

"So when are we going back to your house?" I asked.

"Soon." He wheeled around so our chairs were facing each other. He put his hands on my cheeks and pulled me close. He kissed me right there, out of the blue.

Dennis! Had he done this before?

He leaned in to get even closer, but that pushed my chair, and it wheeled back from him. So he had to use his legs to wheel his chair closer to me again. We cracked up so much that it was hard to kiss.

"I've, uh, never done that before," he said. "I mean, I've kissed a few girls, but never spur-of-the-moment. I usually spend more time planning it out. But I had to do it right away, or I was worried I'd chicken out, and I really didn't want to chicken out."

"Okay." I laughed. "Thanks, I think?"

"Let's do that again later," he said. "But we'll lose the rolling chairs. That just makes the whole operation way too complicated."

"I agree." I smiled and looked up at him. "Dennis, I think you know more about girls than you think you do."

DELICIOUS DISCOVERIES

Kiwi, almond milk, watermelon, pomegranate seeds

JUSTINE

"I made something up," I told Emmett. "So I could leave early and be able to see you again. I mean, it is raining. No one's coming to the truck."

"Okay," he replied, bending down to tie the little shoelace on his Top-Sider. "To your boss? Your uncle or whatever?"

"Uh, yeah." I paused, admiring the top of his head.

"Right." He stood back up. "I only have like a half-hour break today."

"Oh." I looked down at my feet. It felt like this was a rejection, like he was trying to tell me things were over between us.

His eyebrows curved inward like he was confused. "What?"

"Oh, nothing. I thought you were saying you didn't want to hang out."

"No way, dude." He elbowed me, all playful.

I smiled. "Okay, well, in that case, what can we do in a half hour?"

"You know what we can do," he said, waggling his eyebrows. "Sorry, that sounded creepy. There's this cool bookstore a few blocks away."

"I've lived here my whole life and I didn't know about a bookstore near here."

"It's kind of hidden," he said. "Let's go."

Emmett had one of those giant golf umbrellas, so he opened it and held it over both of us. He was so coördinated that he was able to hold up the umbrella with one hand and put his arm around me at the same time. He seemed like the strongest person in the world, like he could handle anything, like nothing was ever a big deal for him.

We walked a few blocks until we got to this teeny, tiny bookstore with two red Adirondack chairs out front. Inside, books were stacked from floor to ceiling on wooden shelves. It smelled dusty. I twitched my nose but I wasn't able to hold in a sneeze.

"Most of our books are used," the owner said, talking to us from the back. "I try to keep it as clean as possible, but ya know . . ."

"It's okay," I said. "Just allergies."

"Hey, Frank," Emmett said. "This is Justine."

Frank tipped his head and then started organizing a stack of papers next to an old-fashioned cash register.

"Frank's the owner," Emmett whispered.

"Did you know him before? Or you just met Frank when you came here this summer?" I asked Emmett.

"I just met him. But he's my buddy."

It seemed like Emmett was one of those people who became "buddies" with everyone he met. In a way, that made me feel less special, but in another way, it made me like him even more.

"Come with me." He pulled my hand, and everything felt so romantic—the smell of old books, the creaky floors, the door-chime jingle when someone went in or out. But then I felt another sneeze coming on. I tried to get a tissue but there wasn't enough time.

I sneezed on Emmett's hand.

There was visible proof.

I wanted to run away and call this a loss, and never see him again. Oh, well. It was good while it lasted.

But then he laughed. "Um, you just sneezed on me."

"I am *so* sorry," I said, reaching into my bag for that little purse pack of tissues that was impossible to find in my black hole of a tote. "So so so sorry."

"It's okay." He winked. I'd never seen him wink before. To be honest, he didn't seem like much of a winker, but somehow he made it work. "I can handle it."

"I am so so sorry. Here, let me help." I finally found the tissues and wiped his hand.

"You sneezed on me," he said again, mostly joking.

"I know. That's like pretty much the grossest thing that could've happened."

He stayed quiet for a second, like he was thinking. "Nah, it's not."

"No?"

We walked through the store, and he started spinning the little rack of twenty-five-cent paperbacks.

"You could've thrown up on me," he suggested. "That would have been grosser."

"Give it time, dude." I smiled. "Give it time."

He elbowed me. "Good one."

Emmett walked away from me and started searching in one section of the store. I wasn't sure what he was looking for, but I didn't really mind not knowing. I didn't even mind the dustiness or the fact that I'd sneeze every few minutes.

"Here," he said a little while later. He handed me a paperback with yellowing pages and a slightly ripped cover. It was by an author I'd never heard of and the title was hard to pronounce. The words seemed made up.

I looked at it for a minute or two, and then he said, "This is one of my favorites. Will you read it? I think you'd really like it."

I didn't have the heart to tell him that science fiction was so not my thing. I barely made it through the first Harry Potter. I never admitted that to anyone, and I wasn't planning on telling him.

"Sure, I'd love to," I said.

He took the book back. "Let me buy it for you."

It was two dollars, but it felt like he was buying me a piece of expensive jewelry. A gift was a gift, and I'd never gotten a gift from a boy before. This was something he cared about, something he loved. He wanted me to read it. He wanted to share it with me. Maybe he kind of hoped I'd love it too?

Maybe we'd love the same thing, and be able to talk about it, and dissect it together.

Emmett paid for the book and we chatted with Frank for a few more minutes. Then Emmett looked at the clock above the door and said, "I gotta get back."

"Are you gonna get in trouble?" I asked as we sprinted toward the bank.

"I hope not," he said, letting go of my hand and leaning in for a quick kiss.

We were stopped at the corner in front of a place called York Deli. It had always been one of those shady places in town that seemed to be a relic from the past. I wasn't sure anyone actually went there anymore.

He put his hands on my shoulders. "I'm gonna leave you here. Get a BLT. I promise you it'll be the best you've ever had." He nodded, trying to get me to agree. "And let me know what you think about that book."

"I'm not a fast reader," I admitted.

"That's okay." He smiled and started running toward the bank. "Take your time. You know where to find me."

SKINNY-DIP

Celery, cherries, kale, blueberries, ice

MIA

We sat on the couch in Dennis's den. My thighs were sweating onto the leather. The more I thought about the fact that I was sweating, the worse it became. I tried to think cool thoughts. Snow days. Blizzards. The freezer in the back of the shop.

Nothing worked.

All I could do was pray that he'd get up and go to the kitchen to get us a drink. Then I'd be able to stand up and dry the sweat on the couch with the sleeve of my cardigan.

I wasn't even sure why I'd brought a cardigan. It was ninety-five degrees outside at six in the evening. But I was grateful I had it because I needed to mop up the sweat.

I'd felt pretty bold back in the snow cone shop, when we were kissing on the rolling desk chairs. I'd even put my arms around his neck, and I'd tried to kiss his ear and stuff.

I wasn't good at this. I knew I wasn't good at it. He knew I wasn't good at it.

But I was trying, and that was something. Effort counted when it came to this stuff, right?

But now, at his house, I felt panicky, like all I wanted to do was get out of there. My stomach hurt and my cheeks itched, like I was breaking out in hives.

I wanted to leave this house and never see Dennis again.

I thought I'd be excited that we had the whole place to ourselves. I'd even brought the navy one-piece I'd worn to Adia Montgomery's party. I was all prepped for the hot tub. I wondered if skinny-dipping was an option . . . but did people really skinny-dip in hot tubs? Was that even safe? I'd planned to do a quick Google at some point, but I hadn't had the chance yet.

But now I didn't want to go in the hot tub or do any of what we'd talked about.

How come everything felt so much easier when it was late at night and you were on the phone, not looking at the person? I'd get all hyped up and excited about it. I was sure I'd be able to handle it. And then I'd get to the time and place and freak out.

I wondered if everyone was like this and they just didn't admit it.

"You okay?" Dennis asked.

He wiped his palms on his jeans. I should have asked him the same thing.

"I'm fine," I said. "Are you okay?"

He nodded. "Yup."

"Dennis, we don't have to do anything major," I blurted out, not even realizing what I was saying. "I mean, I know we only kissed once. And I don't know what you were thinking . . . but I just thought I'd mention that."

He kept nodding. "Yeah, okay. I wasn't sure what you were thinking . . . but I think we should take it slow."

"We don't even have to hook up again," I said. "I mean, we can just hang out. . . ."

"I'm just so nervous," Dennis said, not looking at me. "I don't want to mess this up."

"I'm nervous too," I admitted. "And I never admit when I'm nervous. I always try to play it cool. But I think it's easier to just admit it."

My phone was ringing in my bag across the room, but I was too scared to get up. I didn't want to reveal the sweat puddle that was underneath me.

So I just sat there. We both heard the phone ringing. That only made the situation more awkward.

"I'm gonna get us something to drink," he said finally. "Do you drink wine?"

I tried not to laugh at that. "Do you?"

I didn't drink wine. Right then, I didn't want to drink at all. I mean, a root beer or maybe a Sprite would have been good. But more than anything, I wanted Dennis off that couch. I needed to dry myself off.

When he went into the kitchen, I mopped up the sweat droplets on the couch as quickly as I could. I was grateful they didn't leave a mark on the leather. I tried to air out my armpits near the air-conditioning vent. I scurried over to my bag to check my phone.

I had a missed call and a text from Justine.

Justine: Where are you? Seth just messaged Katie FROM LONDON about hanging out when he's back. He said he was thinking about her . . . We need to plan this out ASAP.

Shit. Okay. I couldn't get into a long back-and-forth with her while Dennis was in the next room.

I wrote back to Justine:

Mia: Call you later. Don't write back yet.

And then Dennis came back to the couch with two glasses of white wine in these fancy champagne glasses. They looked like something adults would use if they were having the dean of a college over for dinner or something.

"This is way fancy, Dennis," I said, laughing a little behind my hand.

"It's all I could find." He shrugged.

We both sipped our wine and then put the glasses down.

"I have to admit something," he said. "I don't really like wine."

"Me neither." I cracked up. "Why are we doing this?"

I waited for him to say something—an inspirational quote, a fact about a losing vice-presidential candidate. But he just sat there. This wasn't the Dennis I knew in the shop. This was like some completely different Dennis who was about to have a panic attack.

"Hey, Dennis. I have a crazy idea. Ready?"

He scratched his head. "Yeah?"

"Let's bake cookies!" I said. "Do you have ingredients? We can always go get some. Come on. It'll be fun!"

I always avoided suggesting sweets or French fries or going out for meals and stuff like that with Seth. I didn't want him to think *Should you really be eating that?* But it wasn't like that with Dennis. I wasn't sure why; I just didn't worry about it in the same way.

Dennis opened his mouth to speak and then hesitated. "I've never baked cookies before," he admitted.

"What?" I gasped. "Never?"

How can you have gone your entire life, all seventeen years of it, without ever baking cookies?

He shook his head. "Nope. Let's do it. I'll get my keys."

As soon as we were outside in the driveway, things felt easier between us. Maybe the fresh air helped. A change of scenery. We were talking again, and laughing. And when we got in the car, Dennis turned up the radio.

It was already on, set to Lite FM.

"I think we're alone now," I sang along, using a flashlight I found in the cup holder as a microphone.

He grabbed it away from me and started singing too. *"Doesn't seem to be anyone arou-ound."*

I loved that he didn't even try to pretend he liked hippie jam bands or hard metal or rap. He listened to Lite FM and didn't even try to hide it.

He knew all the words, too.

REAL APPEAL

Banana, cantaloupe, grapefruit, coconut water

JUSTINE

Seth was back from London and I knew it was go time. It was already the middle of August and summer was winding down. Things were quiet at the truck. Little Leagues were over, camps had ended, and so many Bridgefield families were away on vacation.

I sat at my desk, trying to map out a plan in my head. I had ideas about where we should meet—the ice cream place that had just opened up. He'd mentioned once that he was eating rocky road out of the container, so it was safe to assume that he liked ice cream. I mean, everyone liked ice cream.

Or we could meet at the diner, because people always went to the diner, and it was the most obvious and common place to meet. It would seem like a normal suggestion, and not like we were trying too hard to be creative.

I'd ask Mia when she got here.

Every time I thought about the actual meeting, it felt like someone was scraping out the insides of my stomach with a dentist's pick.

We were going to do this because I'd said we were going to do this. But I wasn't sure if that was a good enough reason.

I twisted my eyebrows, trying to calm down, and then my anxiety made me so tired that I had to get into my bed.

I crawled under the covers for a quick power nap.

I heard knocks on my door, and I wasn't sure how long I'd been asleep.

"Justie?" I heard.

It was Mia. She was the only one in the world who called me Justie. Alexis sometimes did, but more in a poking-fun kind of way. But Mia had called me Justie since kindergarten, and I loved it. When you had a nickname, it really felt like people cared about you, like they knew you.

"Come in," I mumbled.

"You okay?" she asked. She sat down on the edge of my bed.

I nodded, rubbing the tired from my eyes.

"Your mom's asleep on the couch," she told me. "But the kitchen door was open. I rang the bell three times but no one answered. I hope it's okay that I came in."

"Mia. Come on."

"What?"

"Of course it's okay that you came in."

She looked at me for a moment like she had more to say, but

she stayed quiet. After a second or two, she lay down next to me. Sometimes I wondered if all best friends did this. It wasn't like I was going to take a survey of every best-friend duo in the universe to find out if cuddling in bed together was something they did. But maybe it was really weird. Or maybe at some point we'd veered off the path of best-friendship and veered onto the path of sisterhood. Sisters probably cuddled in bed together all the time.

"Tonight's the night," I said a few minutes later.

"Really?" Mia asked.

I wanted to smack her, even though I was hesitant too. "He's back from London, right?"

She nodded. "All right, let's do it. But let's wait until later in the conversation to really bring it up, okay?"

"Well, duh." I got off the bed and walked over to my desk. "We're not just gonna say hi and then set up a meeting time. We have to ease into it."

We sat down in our usual spots at my desk. He was logged in, but on his phone.

"He's out," Mia said. "Has anyone posted about anything going on tonight? Any parties?"

I leaned back and put my feet up. "He could be, like, out to dinner with his great-aunt."

"She's dead," Mia replied matter-of-factly.

I laughed at that because I wasn't really referring to a great-aunt specifically.

"It's not funny," Mia said.

But then I saw her cover her mouth, and she was laughing too. And I'll admit—it was absurd that we were laughing about a dead great-aunt, but it was kind of funny, too.

Katie: Hey

We stared at the computer for a minute or two, waiting to see if Seth was going to write back.

Seth: Hey. I'm out. Can I catch you later?

I felt all the energy being pulled out of us. It was good that he took the time to respond, but it meant our meeting wasn't happening tonight. And if it didn't happen tonight, what if it never happened? What if we chickened out?

The closer it got, the more nervous I felt, and the more I realized we were doing something completely mean and unhinged.

"Don't respond right away," Mia said. "It looks too desperate. Like we're just sitting here waiting for him to write to us."

"Well, we are," I said. "But that's okay. I mean, we know what we're doing."

I wondered what Emmett was doing then. I wondered what it would be like when this was all over and we weren't spending all our time on it. I imagined it would be the kind of feeling like after you take a really important test. You're almost a little sad it's over; you're tempted to look at your flash cards again. But there's also that feeling of relief. Like, *It's done. We survived. It's all in the past now.*

After we had waited a good ten minutes, I leaned over the keyboard and wrote back to Seth.

Katie: Sure

"That's it?" Mia raised her eyebrows.

"You said not to make it look like we were desperate, just sitting here, yada yada . . ."

We were having a heated debate about why trying too hard and making it look like you try too hard is the kiss of death, when the screen flashed and we saw that Seth had written something else.

Seth: Actually, can I ask you something? Girl's perspective again . . . you're good at that.

We looked at each other. Maybe the night was picking up.

Katie: Sure, shoot. And thanks. ☺

"That was a tiny bit cheesy, but I'll let it go," Mia said.

"Katie's a little cheesy," I reminded her. "Remember?"

"True."

Seth: I'm at this party, and my friends are trying to convince me to hook up with this girl from our school. She's kind of terrible, though. If I hook up with her, am I destined for hell? Will she ruin my life?

"Oh my God!" Mia shrieked. "See, I told you he wasn't out to dinner with a great-aunt! But who is he talking about?"

"Ummm." I thought for a second. I couldn't believe Seth put so much thought into his random hookups. But then again, after the whole Adia thing, I guess he had to. I guess he was learning his lessons. That was a good thing. "Fran Pucillo?"

"Ew," Mia replied. "No." She paused for a second. "Is she a V or an NV?"

"Total NV," I declared. "Last summer with Edward Tonno. Last winter break with Dylan Simms . . . I could go on."

Mia rolled her eyes. "No, thanks."

The Seth conversation was just sitting there, lingering in the air. What were we going to say to that?

Mia leaned over and started typing.

Katie: Don't do it. Honestly, it's not worth it. A girl like that could ruin your life . . .

I pulled Mia's hands away from the keyboard. I had no idea what she was doing.

"What?" she asked.

"Just sounds eerie," I said. "Is what we're doing going to ruin his life? Were you foreshadowing about us?"

She looked at me, her eyebrows curved inward. "No, I don't think so."

We stared at each other.

"I mean, we're not ruining his life forever, but for a little while."

She paused. "He ruined my life for a little while, too? Nothing is permanent, right?"

"Right," I answered. I wasn't sure if she meant that her life was no longer ruined, that she felt okay now. Over him, even. I had so many questions to ask, and so many doubts, that I kept them all locked up in my head.

If I let them out, I feared everything would unravel.

We had to meet him soon, finish our project before I really had time to think about what we were doing. If I gave it too much thought, I would probably see that this was the most evil thing in the world.

JUST PEACHY

Peaches, vanilla frozen yogurt

MIA

Seth: This party is super lame. And I really want to get out of here. Want to be my excuse to leave?

"Umm, look at this." I covered my face, showing Justine my phone. We'd moved away from the computer and we were watching a *Real Housewives* marathon on her bed.

"This is happening," Justine said. "This is actually happening. Right now."

"Can we go out now, though?" I asked her, sitting up. "I mean, your parents. And it's almost ten at night. What should we do? What should we do?" I tied my hair back into a ponytail.

"Let's just go," she said, getting up from the bed. "My mom is probably asleep. My dad won't really notice."

"Wait." I grabbed her hand. "We didn't even respond yet."

"Oh, right."

We went back to the computer because it was easier than typing on our phones.

Katie: Ummm . . .

Seth: Are you free to meet up tonight?

"Why are we stalling?" I asked Justine.

"Well, we need to make him work for it. At least a little bit." She looked at me. "He can't think Katie's just sitting around waiting for him."

Katie: Give me twenty minutes. Let's meet at the Oakridge Diner. Just in case you don't recognize me from the pictures, you'll know it's me because I'm wearing a red shirt.

Oakridge was the town next to Bridgefield, and it made the most sense to meet there. It was close enough to where Seth lived, and close to where Katie "lived," but we probably wouldn't know anyone there.

Yeah, we wanted to embarrass him. But this whole project was also a little embarrassing for us, too. Did we really want spectators? Not at all.

Seth: Cool. I'll have a Yankees cap on.

"We need to go," I said. My whole body was shaking. I couldn't control my hands or my leg twitches. I kept smoothing my hair down, over and over again. I wished I'd worn something different, but there I was in my rattiest cutoffs; I loved them, but they weren't quite long enough to prevent the chub-rub during long walking periods. The chub-rub was shrinking, thanks to the smoothies, but it was still there.

"We both need to be wearing red shirts," Justine said. "That way it's clear. He knows what we did. He knows we demolished him." She went over to her dresser and grabbed a red V-neck tee and a red tank top. "I'll wear the tee. You wear the tank top. Show off your amazing arms."

"Okay," I said. "Let's just get this over with."

This felt like when we'd have fire drills at school. Sometimes the teachers would tell us in advance, so we'd be waiting for the alarm to go off. But it didn't matter how prepared we were. When the alarm finally did start blaring, we jumped. Completely startled. Always.

Maybe there was never a way to prepare. For anything.

Justine's mom was asleep in the brown recliner, covered by this fuzzy orange blanket they had. I think Justine's grandma had knitted it years and years ago.

"We're going out for a bite," Justine told her dad, not looking at him.

"Okay." He turned around from the computer. "Be careful."

"That was easy," Justine said when we were in the car.

We drove in silence for a while after that. We didn't even listen to music.

"What if we get there first?" I asked.

"We go in and get a booth and order a plate of cheese fries." We were at a red light. She looked at me like it was the most obvious thing in the world. "Duh."

"Duh," I repeated.

"What if he gets there first?" It seemed like I was quizzing her, which I kind of was, because it was comforting for me to know she had this all figured out.

"If he gets there first, we go in, see where he is. Done."

"Done?" I asked.

My heart sank a little then because that would mean it was over. Really, really over. As over as it could possibly be. No more talking late at night. No more finding out his innermost feelings.

There was no coming back from this.

There was nothing after over. Over was the end.

I was ready for it, but it was still so final.

"I can't imagine it will be a very long interaction," Justine said. "But I could be wrong. I mean, maybe he'll think it's super funny and then sit and chat with us."

"You'd let him sit and chat with us?" I asked.

"No. Definitely not."

We pulled into the diner parking lot and I looked for his car. He wasn't there yet.

"We should go in, right?" I asked Justine.

"One second."

"My heart hurts," I said. "But not like it did after the breakup. It's like a physical hurt this time. I feel it in my throat." I put my hand to my chest. "I think I'm having a heart attack."

Justine looked worried. "Really?"

I nodded.

"We should leave, right?" Justine asked. "Maybe this really did go too far. Maybe it was too cruel. Either way, you can't die on me, Mia. You can't die on me!"

I couldn't tell if she was kidding or if she was really worried. I wasn't going to die. Did people know they were going to die before they died?

"I don't think I'm actually going to die," I said. "Honestly."

We got out of the car and stood there in the parking lot, staring at each other, and I wasn't sure what to do. My throat felt tight. It's not every day that you make up a fake person and develop a fake relationship with your ex-boyfriend. It's not every day that the fake relationship gets so intense that you end up meeting face-to-face at a diner.

One thing was for sure: I was never doing this again.

Never. Ever.

JUST BEET IT

Beets, cucumbers, celery, cranberries

JUSTINE

I wanted to back out so badly. I was nauseous and my heartbeats felt uneven. Was that a sign of a stroke?

I wasn't brave. I wasn't daring. I wasn't the kind of girl who came up with plans like this.

I couldn't even remember why I had done this anymore. I wanted to prove something to Mia, but she got the point. She was probably over Seth way long ago, and I was too focused on Katie to even notice it. I wanted to prove something to myself, but I knew the truth all along.

People hurt others. It was a simple fact of life. And even the best revenge plots wouldn't change that.

I didn't need to take it this far. I still hadn't Googled if this was an arrestable offense; I was too nervous to find out the answer.

"Let's go in," I said. "We'll just be at the diner, like, the two of us sharing cheese fries and a vanilla shake, like normal. And he'll show up. And he'll look for Katie. And he may not put two and two together. Ya know?"

I was talking so fast, and I couldn't stop myself. I was ashamed, and embarrassed about what I'd done, and now I couldn't see any way out of it.

"The red shirts," Mia reminded me. "It's pretty clear."

"Right, so maybe we should just leave," I suggested. "Katie disappears. No one knows what happened. . . ."

Mia put her hands on my shoulders. "Justine. Stop."

I needed to be talked off the ledge.

"Let's go in," she said in her soft, trying-to-stay-calm voice. "We started this. We are finishing it."

I'd always heard people say that you never regret things you do; you only regret things you don't do.

But in this case, that wasn't true at all.

I was regretting the things I'd done.

I was regretting everything.

44 THE CURE

Vanilla frozen yogurt, mango sorbet

MIA

We finally went in. The hostess sat us at a booth in the back, and we ordered cheese fries—mozzarella, of course—and a vanilla shake. We sipped our waters while we waited for the food. We played with sugar packets. We doodled on the place mats—rainbows, our initials, stars, hearts—with the complimentary crayons like we were seven years old again.

This wasn't *our* diner, but it was close enough. They were all pretty much the same. Everything felt normal, like all the other nights we'd spent eating cheese fries.

Until it wasn't.

Justine was telling me this story about what happened after Uncle Rick won the lottery, and how every person he'd ever known, pretty much, asked him for money. And at first he gave away a ton, but then it got out of control. I was listening to every word, because I still found the whole thing so fascinating.

And then I heard his voice.

"Oh, I'm just meeting someone here." He sounded nervous, hesitant.

"Take a seat wherever you'd like," the hostess said. Her long nails clicked on the computer keyboard in front of her.

I didn't look over. I couldn't make eye contact with him. Justine was still telling the story. Did she not notice he was here? I kicked her under the table.

Seth walked around a little. I could see him out of the corner of my eye. His Yankees hat. A faded Heinz ketchup T-shirt. That swagger.

I guessed he was trying to get a good spot—a good table for him, and for Katie. Maybe somewhere secluded, somewhere quiet.

He walked right past us, and for a second, I was happy about that. We could see him sitting there, across the diner, waiting forever for Katie to show up. And then he'd feel pathetic. *The girl didn't even show,* he'd think. He would be too sad to even notice us or our red shirts.

And maybe he'd walk out of the diner with his head down.

He'd never know we had anything to do with what had happened

But we'd know the truth.

Sure, there wouldn't be any confrontation. But maybe it would be better that way.

Then he stopped.

I guessed he saw us out of a corner of his eye, too.

It was almost like I could see everything that had happened flash across his brain. I could see him putting the pieces together, one by one.

"Mia?" he said. His voice shook a little bit. I looked up, but after that I froze. I opened my mouth to say *Hi, Seth,* but nothing came out. I sat there with my mouth open.

Justine looked up too. But he didn't say her name. And she didn't say anything either.

In all honesty, it was probably only about five seconds. Five seconds of the three of us staring at each other—well, really Justine and me staring at him, and him staring back at us.

It felt like forever, though. Like time stopped right then and we were all frozen.

"What the—?" He stopped himself, and then he said, "You guys are sick."

I could handle that. Really. I thought he'd walk away, leave the diner, end the whole thing. I was okay with that.

"You're sick," he continued. "Like, seriously deranged. Insane, actually."

We just sat there, listening to him, unable to speak.

I was ready for him to stop.

The waitress came over. "Is everything okay?"

He ignored her. "You guys are insane," he said again and again, his voice getting louder.

Everyone in the diner turned and stared at us. They all looked confused and kind of scared.

"I'm going to need to ask you to leave," the manager said to Seth.

Justine and I looked at the short man in the bulging button-down shirt. We glanced over at Seth.

We covered our mouths with our hands.

Seth stayed there, in front of us, but he quieted down.

We were speechless. I couldn't find a single thing to say. Justine looked down at her place mat. She turned it over to the blank side and folded her arms on the table.

"Forget this," Seth said. "Why am I standing here? Why am I even talking to you two? You're sick!"

"Seth, you seem so upset" was all Justine managed to say. She laughed a little and bit her lip.

I stayed quiet.

The manager put a hand on Seth's shoulder. "I'm not sure what's happening here. But you need to leave now, or I'll have to call the police."

"I'm leaving," Seth said to no one in particular.

We watched him walk away.

Goodbye, Seth.

This was the end.

It took us a long time to get here because I couldn't face it, because I didn't want it to be the end, because I would have done anything to hang on.

But this was it.

We had set him up.

We had humiliated him.

But only a tiny piece of me felt victorious. The rest of me felt humiliated too.

VICTORY DANCE

Lime juice, jalapeños, honey, kiwi

JUSTINE

We stayed to finish the cheese fries.

"Did that really just happen?" Mia asked me. I knew exactly what she meant. It had happened so quickly, and he was literally only in front of us for a minute. It was so fast that it almost seemed like we'd imagined it.

"I think so," I told her.

"So we did it?" she asked.

I nodded and put a napkin over the ketchup blob on my plate.

"Should we feel proud now?" she asked me.

"Yes!" I yelled, and a few people nearby turned around. This was definitely the craziest night the Oakridge Diner had ever seen. "We lured him in, and got him to show up, and we convinced him Katie was a person worth knowing, and he fell for her . . . when it was us all along."

"Right, and I mean, we totally humiliated him," Mia said, kind of like she was trying to convince herself, like she was trying to convince me, too. "Because he was super into her . . ."

"You're one hundred percent, completely over him now, right?" I asked her.

She hesitated and said, "Yes."

Still. After everything that had happened, I wasn't sure she was telling the truth.

I started to wonder if everyone had at least one person in their life, one love, that just crept right into their brain and their heart and stayed there, like, permanently. Maybe because he was her first boyfriend, the first one who paid attention to her, and sought her out, and made her feel like someone.

He didn't take up her whole heart anymore, now he was only a tiny freckle, but he was still there. Maybe he'd always be there.

Maybe no matter what—we could never totally get over that first person.

"I feel like we accomplished what we wanted to accomplish," Mia said. "But I don't feel great. Ya know?"

I nodded. I knew what she meant. I wanted to feel different, but I felt just as shaky as she did. "I know, I mean, it was a psychotic thing to do. We knew that going into it."

"Are we totally evil?" Mia asked me.

I hesitated before I answered. "We're a little evil." I paused. "But here's the thing—we can take something from what we did. We can take something from the fact that he broke your heart, and we got back at him, and you healed!"

Mia nodded and leaned forward on the table like she was listening to me.

"We can help others heal too!"

"Huh?" She moved back. "I don't think we can keep making up fake Internet personalities, Justie."

"Okay, no." I chewed the end of my straw. "We can't, but, like, maybe we can be those people who others go to when they want to get over a breakup. I don't know. We can prove that girls don't need to just take whatever guys throw at them; they can stand up for themselves! We can empower them!"

Mia's eyes bulged. "Okay, I get what you're saying, but . . ."

I played with my straw and tried to turn it into a heart shape. "Here's the thing we need to remember. We did it. We achieved what we wanted to achieve. You didn't just stand by and feel sad all summer. You took action." I slammed my hand on the table. Mia startled.

"What was that?" she asked.

"I'm done with this, Mia!" I yelled. "We did it. We humiliated the crap out of Seth. He hurt you, and we hurt him back. We got him back!"

"We did. I know we did."

"We did a bad thing, but we can make something positive out of it. We can feel awesome about ourselves and how we can learn from our mistakes."

Mia was quiet then, but I knew she was listening.

"Let's just never do that again, obviously, and also feel awesome about ourselves from now on, okay?" I felt like a motivational speaker. So much so that my throat was getting dry and I needed to sip my water. I was fired up. I wanted to stand on the table and tell the whole diner what we'd done. I wanted to tell the whole world what we'd done.

"Is it that easy?" Mia asked. "Even if we feel awesome about ourselves, will we still feel invisible?"

I paused and thought about it. "I think it is that easy. I think if we work at it, it can be that easy."

She waited for me to say more. I slurped the last little bit of milk shake. "We've felt crappy about ourselves for a while. And I'm just done with it. We're awesome."

"We're awesome," she repeated.

"And we can do things! Take action! We don't need to just let stuff happen! I mean, this was a crazy thing, and it wasn't the nicest thing to do to a person. But it just proves that we're capable of so much! We can go to protests and marches and stuff!" I yelled, almost wanting everyone to hear me. "We can do whatever we want to do!"

"Yes, we can!" Mia laughed.

She walked around the table and came to sit next to me on my side of the booth. It was a little awkward, and I think the rest of the people at the diner thought we were some new lesbian couple who was planning to come out any minute. She put her arm around me. "I love you, Justine."

"I love you," I said in a half-jokey voice.

"No, but really," Mia said. She still had her arm around me. She smelled like ketchup. "I really do. I'm so grateful for everything you do for me. And I know I don't always say it. But I am. I really am."

I liked what she was saying, and it made me feel good, but I wanted her to stop. It felt like too much.

"Thanks, Mia. Thanks for saying it."

She finally pulled away and went back to her side of the booth.

We motioned for the waitress that we wanted the check.

We overtipped that night because in some weird way, it felt like Nancy, the middle-aged waitress, was also part of our victory. It felt like everyone at the diner that night was part of our victory.

We walked out to my car.

"He really did show up, though, right?" Mia asked me again.

"He did," I replied.

I was almost positive.

PEACE AND QUIET

Chamomile tea, honey, lemon, whipped yogurt

MIA

Justine dropped me off at home after the diner. We needed to sleep in our own beds that night.

I heard my phone buzz on my night table and had no idea what time it was or what was going on.

"We should tell Justine. I don't like secrets."

Dennis.

"What?" I mumbled.

"Are you asleep?" he asked me. I was surprised he couldn't tell. There was a huge difference between awake Mia and asleep Mia.

"Yeah. I fell asleep watching TV, I guess."

"I want to tell Justine how I feel about you . . . how you feel about me. I want us to be a thing."

My heart pounded. *A thing?* Was I ready to be a thing with Dennis?

"Can we discuss this tomorrow?" I paused. "I'm really asleep, Dennis. I'm so sorry."

"Oh, uh, okay."

I fell asleep again while holding the phone.

"Bye, Mia."

"Bye."

The next morning, I woke up and only had a vague recollection of the Dennis conversation. I also had a text from Seth.

> I don't know what the hell you and Justine thought you were doing but it was totally messed up. I thought you were a normal girl. And I'm sorry we broke up. But that's just mad crazy. I want to tell everyone how insane you are, but I won't. I'll keep it between us. You owe me one, though.

I owed him one? Yeah, right.

Seth was shrinking. From an elephant to a poodle to a frog.

He was a mosquito now.

I needed to get rid of him completely. Once and for all.

If I was ever going to figure out how I felt about Dennis, I needed to give him a fair shake, a true chance, one hundred percent focus. This whole time, he'd been there, and I'd been into him, but Seth had been there too.

Justine picked me up on the way to work.

"I've been thinking about what you said," I told her as I got into the car.

"Yeah? *We're never gonna survive, unless we get a little crazy,*" she sang along to the playlist.

"I think that may be the theme of our summer, by the way." I looked at her. "That song."

"Oh, yeah." She shimmied her shoulders. "You're right! Wait, so what were you thinking about?"

I turned the music down a little. "Just that we are awesome. And we do need to feel great about ourselves." I sipped my water. I was dreaming about the kale-mango-raspberry-coconut smoothie I was going to make as soon as we got to the shop. I didn't have a name for this one yet. It was going to have something to do with revenge. "But I still feel guilty about what we did."

"Me too," Justine added. "But I need to admit something."

My insides twisted. "What?"

"I was so tempted to log in as Katie last night," she said. "But I didn't. Obviously. And then I felt kind of sad. Katie's dead."

"She is dead," I replied. "But she was never really alive."

"She kind of was alive to me."

I knew what she meant. "I know, because, like, when we were Katie, we could say stuff we wouldn't normally say."

Justine slow-nodded. "I know. We were brave when we were Katie."

"We're still going to be brave. As ourselves," I replied. "Maybe that's what we need to take from this. Whenever we feel uncertain, we can channel Katie in real life!"

She stopped at a red light and pulled her hair up into a bun. "Yes! Whenever we're feeling shaky or unsure, we'll think *Channel Katie.* We'll remind each other of that in moments of panic!"

"Exactly!" I stretched out my legs. "Seth texted me, by the way."

"And?" she asked.

"He just said we were so messed up, basically. And that he could totally tell everyone how insane we are. But he won't."

"Of course he won't!" Justine yelled, and slammed on the brakes at the stop sign. I grabbed on to the door handle. "Because that would humiliate him, too. Do you see what I'm saying?"

I nodded. "Yeah, totally. But that's why your plan was so brilliant, because he was humiliated. He can't tell anyone!"

"I kind of want to tell people," Justine admitted. "It was terrible but I'm also proud of it. It's like this black-and-white cookie of a thing, you know?"

I shifted in my seat. "Exactly. I feel like we accomplished something, but it was a bad thing to accomplish."

"How can we stop feeling guilty about it?" Justine asked me. "The whole time we were doing it, all I could think about was getting him to show up and think Katie was real, but I didn't realize how crappy I'd feel after it happened."

I chewed the inside of my cheek. "Yeah, exactly. It's like a twinge of crappiness after the sweetness of success."

"So poetic." Justine laughed. "Strawberry-vanilla smoothie with a kick of sour lemon that hits you at the end?"

"We can call it When Life Gives You Lemons?" I suggested, giggling.

"Yes!" Justine screamed.

I did a little dance in my seat. "Right! When life gives you lemons, you make up a fake online personality and get revenge on your ex-boyfriend, and create a smoothie business, and basically take charge!"

"Yeah," she said. "We need to keep reminding ourselves that the Katie thing wasn't our only success this summer. Hello, secret smoothie business!"

"I know," I replied, shifting in my seat. "And that kind of happened out of the blue. Imagine what we can do when we're actually, like, trying?"

"World domination!" Justine yelled.

We cracked up the whole way to work, making up new life mantras, singing along to the playlist.

I loved Justine and me. I prayed silently that things would always stay the way they were in that moment.

WAKE UP AND RISE UP

Spinach, kale, mango, a touch of hot sauce, watermelon

JUSTINE

We'd sold over fifty smoothies the next day and we would have sold more, but we ran out of ingredients.

"I'm disappointed," one lady told us. "I needed my Radical Change today. I'm going through a divorce, ya know?"

We tried to be sympathetic. "Our distributor was closed this week due to a family emergency," I lied. "So things have been a little crazy."

She nodded like that almost made things better, but not quite. "Well, I guess that can happen. I'll try to find my Radical Change somewhere else, I suppose. . . ."

I met Emmett at the bank after we'd returned the truck, and I told him about all the customers.

"These ladies really need you," Emmett said after I told him the story about the ladies from the Temple Sinai Sisterhood who were obsessed with Wake Up and Rise Up, our newest creation. They told us they were letting the rabbi know about it because it felt so spiritual to them.

Spiritual Smoothies could be our offshoot business . . . catering to synagogues, churches, mosques . . . I made a mental note to think about that at a later time.

"I guess they do need us." I propped my foot up on his knee to tie my shoe. "How weird is that, though?"

"Eh." He shrugged. "Adults are wack. They're pretty much just big children."

"You think?" I sat back in my chair. We were in the break room, and I definitely wasn't supposed to be here. But summer was winding down, and Emmett was leaving soon anyway. And let's be honest—his dad was some major guy on the corporate side. He could pretty much do whatever he wanted.

"I think so." Emmett looked at me and I wanted to pull his face in and keep it in my pocket forever. I knew it was creepy and possessive, but more than anything, I just wanted him to stay with me.

"So you started to tell me something crazy happened last night," he said, leaning his head on my shoulder.

"Okay, so are you ready for this?" I asked him. I had to tell him. I was nervous about how he was going to respond, but I just had to. The story was bubbling out of me.

"Um, yes?"

"Okay, so, right at the end of school Mia's douchebag boyfriend cheated on her at a party we were at, and then broke up with her,"

I said. "So I did what any sensible best friend would do. I made up a fake online person, and stalked him, and got him to fall in love with the fake girl and want to meet her, and then he actually showed up at the diner. After the whole summer of Katie talking to him. I think he, like, loved her in a way . . . or was falling in love with her."

As I talked, I still felt that heart-racing victorious pride feeling alongside the twinge of embarrassment and creepiness.

"Who's Katie?" Emmett asked.

"The girl I made up," I said, clenching my teeth.

"So basically you Catfished your friend's ex-boyfriend and he fell for it?"

I nodded.

"For real? You're only just telling me about this now? And it's been going on all summer?" His eyes were squinty. "You're kidding, right?"

"No," I said, regretting telling him. He was about to break up with me right then. He knew I was totally messed up. "It's all true."

He jerked his head back, eyebrows raised. "That's pretty intense."

"Yeah, intense and totally screwed up. I know that. But I couldn't just let Seth do that to Mia. He couldn't, like, just get away with it."

"Whoa, dude." I liked when he called me dude. I wasn't sure why. I wanted to be hot, feminine, someone he wanted to make out with. But at the same time, when he called me dude, it felt like he *knew* me. "It's psychotic, but it came from a good place. It's pretty bold how much you wanted to help Mia."

"It's bold, yeah. It was, like, I had to do something." I looked over at him. "Situations are never just one thing, ya know?"

"Never." He put his hands on my knees and leaned in, and we put our foreheads together. It made me feel connected to him. Like our brains were intertwined, like *we* understood each other.

And that was pretty much all I ever wanted.

Emmett called me later that night, which was odd and caught me off guard. We weren't phone talkers. We texted sometimes, but we were more the in-person types. Everything that happened between us happened face-to-face, forehead-to-forehead.

"Justine?" he said after I answered, like he wasn't sure it was me on the phone. That was so strange because it was my cell phone and no one else would answer it. Did I look like the kind of person who would leave her cell phone unattended?

"Yeah? Hey."

"I was gonna come by and tell you this in person, but I didn't want to wait that long to talk to you." He paused. "I just found out I'm leaving a week earlier than I thought."

"Wait, what?" I turned down the TV. "You're leaving next week?"

He hesitated and then said, "Yeah. Friday."

I sniffled.

"Don't cry," he said.

"Oh, I'm not," I replied, because I wasn't crying. I felt like crying, but I wouldn't actually do that on the phone with him. And then the notion that he thought I was crying felt so sweet that I actually did start to cry. And then I thought how funny it was that I'd actually started crying when I'd never expected to cry, and I started laughing.

"I don't even know what's going on," he said. "Girls are nutty."

"We are," I said.

"I wanted to tell you as soon as I found out," he said.

"Okay." My mind was spinning. Emmett was leaving. I'd known he would leave eventually, but this was sooner than I thought. I wasn't ready.

"I want to meet Mia before I go," he said. "She's your best friend and you spent all summer helping her and doing crazy stuff. I want to meet her."

"Okay," I said.

I wasn't sure how to tell him that Mia didn't know he existed.

SUMMER LOVIN'

Strawberries, raspberries, kale, nectarines, a sprinkle of chili powder

MIA

We sat on the love seat in Dennis's backyard after Uncle Rick and Dennis's mom had gone to bed. The bottom was wicker and the cushions were nice enough to be on an indoor couch.

"This backyard is so fancy," I said. "I kind of feel like we're at a resort."

"Yeah, they drag these cushions in every night, in case it rains." He shook his head. "They need to hire some resort staff."

I giggled a little, and yeah, we were talking about outdoor furniture, quite possibly the most boring conversation in the world, but it felt okay, not forced or anything.

There was only a slight breeze so the air felt warm and thick. Dennis had made some fruit punch and we sipped it out of tall glasses with colorful straws.

We sat side by side, but then he inched closer. He put his arm around me, and he started kissing my cheek. And maybe it was the breeze or the way he stroked my hair or the way he smelled like fruit punch, which sounds disgusting but actually wasn't. And then he said, "Mia, you're so beautiful."

And the way he said it—I believed him.

And soon we were kissing. I looked up to Uncle Rick's bedroom window to make sure they were really asleep and the lights were off. And then I looked back at Dennis. He pulled me up onto his lap. I wrapped my arms around his neck.

"I know about your smoothies," he said, pulling back.

Okay, not what I expected to hear from the boy I was making out with.

"What?" I cracked up.

"Your smoothies. You and Justine. You have your own side smoothie business?" He half-smiled. "You're very popular."

"Oh. Right." I chewed my bottom lip. "Our smoothies."

"People post pictures of themselves with the smoothies all the time, they put the location and everything." He smiled. "Did you really think it was going to stay a secret? I've known for weeks now."

"Um." I half-smiled and kissed his cheek.

"Don't worry," he said. "Your secret's safe with me, and I don't think Rick's savvy enough to figure it out. He doesn't do social media." He looked up toward the window. "And ya know, I'd never rat out my girlfriend."

I smiled. So this was happening.

"You are my girlfriend, right?" he asked. "I mean, I hope you are. . . . Is there a way for me to ask you to be my girlfriend? Or it's just assumed? Like after a certain amount of time . . . or something?"

I shrugged. "I have no idea. But I can be your girlfriend." I kissed him again. "And thanks for keeping our secret. I mean, it may not always be a secret, but for now it is. Who knows?"

If anyone had told me at the beginning of the summer that this was how things were going to be in August, I never would have believed them. Never ever in a million years.

But right then, it felt like everything had worked out exactly how it was meant to.

I could be myself with Dennis.

I felt happy.

I felt lighter, too. I'd lost about six pounds from drinking the smoothies and not snacking as much as I had been, but that wasn't the only reason.

I didn't have the Seth stuff weighing me down. I'd gotten rid of all the obsessive thoughts, and the memory slideshows, and the stalking.

I'd put the pen away in the memory box in my closet.

It had taken so long, but I finally felt free.

THE COLD TRUTH

Crushed ice, frozen blueberries, frozen vanilla yogurt

JUSTINE

"Okay, we need to talk," I said to Mia as soon as she got into my car.

I planned to get right to the point and tell her about Emmett. I'd explain how it was hard to open up about him because it was so new and I was unsure about where it was going. Hopefully she'd understand and not be mad at me. I had to be done with the secrets and the lies. I decided that was going to be my New Year's resolution for senior year: Be upfront and honest. And tell the truth all the time.

"What's up?" Mia asked. She was distracted, looking at her phone. I tried to peek over at what she was doing, but it was too hard to see.

"So I haven't told you some stuff," I said.

"Ummm." Mia looked over at me, but I was driving so I

couldn't make eye contact with her. Maybe that was easier. Maybe it was harder to tell the truth when you had to look them in the eyes and see their reaction. Maybe life in general was harder face-to-face, and the Katie experiment was proof of that. Seth and Katie talked so easily, so quickly over Messenger because they didn't have to look at each other.

"So, you know how I've been going to the bank and depositing all the money?"

She nodded. "Please don't tell me you spent it all on some really intense tattoo or something."

"What? Ew. No. You know I hate tattoos."

"I know," Mia replied. "But you're scaring me."

"It's nothing like that. It's kind of a long—"

"Just tell me!" Mia screeched, turning down the music.

"Okay, so I met this guy on one of the first days I went to deposit the money," I told her. "And we, like, hit it off right away."

"Yeah?" Mia put down her phone. "So far this is better than I thought it was going to be."

"It was hot, Mi," I continued. "We hooked up in the safe-deposit box room!"

"What?" She screeched again. "Are you serious? And you didn't tell me."

"I know. . . ." We finally got to a red light and made eye contact. "I was scared to tell you, because I kind of thought it was going to end. And I didn't want to, like, bring anyone else into it if it was just gonna end. Ya know?"

She tilted her head to the side. "Not really. But okay. Go on."

"But it didn't end," I said. "We've been hooking up all summer."

"Justine!" she yelled. "Pull over. This is way too crazy a story for you to just keep driving. Come on. It's not even safe, really."

So I drove into the parking lot of the ice cream place we always went to after band concerts.

"You kept this from me all summer?" Mia asked, staring at me. "I don't get it. I feel so weird now."

"I'm sorry. I know it's so crazy," I admitted. "I honestly thought he was gonna end it because whatever, I have zero hooking-up experience . . . and no boys ever like me."

"Justine," she whispered. "Come on. Elliott Chaffler. You totally rejected him."

"Okay, but aside from Elliott Chaffler, who just wanted to get some on the Outdoor Ed trip . . ." I giggled. "I just didn't expect this to become anything real. But it is. I mean, I like him. And he likes me."

"That's awesome," Mia said. "You're starting senior year with a boyfriend. That's huge. You probably already have a prom date. This is amazing."

"Well, not really. He lives in Boston with his mom. He was just here for the summer, because he was staying with his dad," I told her. "And I thought he was gonna be here a few more weeks. But he's actually leaving, like, in a few days."

"Oh." She looked down at her flip-flops. "That sucks. I'm sorry."

I could tell she was still a little mad that I hadn't told her before.

But underneath that, she did feel bad that my first-ever boyfriend was leaving and that he didn't live here to begin with.

"Why'd you decide to tell me now?" she asked.

"Well, he's leaving, and I couldn't keep it from you anymore."

"Oh" was all she said for a few minutes. "Well, I'm happy for you. But can you please just tell me stuff from now on?"

I sniffled a little, like I was actually going to cry. I wasn't sure what was happening to me. It felt like my emotions were taking up the whole car.

"And speaking of telling people stuff . . ." Mia's voice trailed off. "Uncle Rick. Are we telling him or no? Summer is gonna end soon."

I shrugged. "I don't know what to do."

"Actually," Mia said, "I don't think we should tell him. The only thing he really wants to hear is that his snow cones were a huge success. And they sold pretty well! There's money in the account. We don't need to take that away from him by talking about our business."

Maybe she was right. "I get what you're saying."

There were reasons for telling the truth, a lot of reasons, actually. There were probably more reasons for telling the truth than for not telling the truth. But I guess there were times when lying was okay, too. There were times when lying was actually the right thing to do.

OUT IN THE OPEN

Raspberries, blueberries, agave nectar, kale

MIA

We kept driving, and we were almost at work when I couldn't take it anymore. All this talk about lying made me burst with guilt and anxiety. Enough was enough.

"Justine . . . I have to tell you something, too," I started.

"Yeah?" She'd been singing along to the radio. *"There was only you and me. We were young and wild and free."*

I wondered if she was thinking about that Emmett kid. I wanted to meet him. I wanted him to stay. I wanted Justine to be happy like this all the time.

"I've been hooking up with Dennis," I blurted out.

"What?" she screeched. "I thought you guys just quizzed each other on losing candidates, or whatever?"

I was going to have to force her to pull over again, but we were almost there. I wasn't used to this much commotion so early in the morning. I needed my smoothie.

"I'm sorry," I said. "Well, it started out that I'd complain to him about Seth. But then Dennis just made me feel so . . . great about myself, and beautiful. And it just became a thing."

"He's my stepcousin, Mia."

Justine looked like she was about to barf. I cleaned out the inside of an old smoothie cup I found lying on the floor of her car, just in case.

"I know. And I'm sorry." I mushed my face together, half-scared she was going to barf and half-scared she was going to yell at me. "It's not like he's your biological cousin, though?"

"Ew. Ew. Ew." She said that word over and over again. I guessed this wasn't the time to tell her that Dennis was actually pretty good at hooking up, and that he knew about our smoothies. I'd save that for another time.

We drove the rest of the way in silence, and I hoped she was warming up to the idea, or at least getting used to it.

Finally we were at the shop. Uncle Rick was washing the outside of the truck. He was wearing a tank top. I hoped the grossness of that image would wipe away Justine's icky feelings about Dennis and me.

"Hey, Uncle Rick," Justine said.

"Oh, hello to my favorite salesladies!" He saluted us. "Go on in, we have to discuss your last day . . . and when we're closing up for the season."

Dennis was inside the shop, on the computer, tweeting depressing quotes about the end of summer on the Mobile Cones Twitter account.

I read over his shoulder, breathing in his Old Spice deodorant. Why did it smell so good?

What good is the warmth of summer,
without the cold of winter to give it sweetness.
JOHN STEINBECK

"Nice," I said. "And totally true."

He shrugged. "I found it on one of your quote pages." He kissed my hand when Justine and Uncle Rick weren't looking.

"Listen up," Uncle Rick said. "I just need to thank all three of you. To be honest, I wasn't sure we could make a go of this snow cone business. It was a dream of mine, but I have a lot of dreams, and many don't pan out." He looked down at his shoes—old worn-in Reeboks; he could clearly afford another pair. "But I'm thrilled with how everything has turned out. And I have you all to thank." He paused like he was giving an Oscar speech. "So thank you."

"You're welcome, Uncle Rick." I smiled.

What if I ended up marrying Dennis one day? And Uncle Rick became my stepdad-in-law? Eventually I'd have to tell him about the smoothies. I'd be like, *Want to hear a really crazy story about the summer I worked at Simply Snow Cones?* And I'd tell him everything—about the lady and the kale, about when Dennis and I became something. Maybe I'd even tell him about Katie.

We'd laugh about it because it would all be so far in the past that none of it would matter and all of it would seem funny.

I liked to picture myself then—older, smarter, more sophisticated, even.

But I didn't want to rush it, really.

For once, I was pretty happy with the way things were.

HEARTBREAK HEALER

Raspberries, watermelon, mango sorbet, apricot

MIA

"So this is the famous Mia," Emmett said as he sat down in the booth at the diner.

"I don't know about that." I laughed.

"Mia, Emmett. Emmett, Mia." Justine moved her hand back and forth, introducing us. "Sorry it's taken so long for you two to meet."

"Apology accepted," I said.

"Same," Emmett added, looking at the menu. "So what's good here? The filet of sole? Or the complete Thanksgiving dinner? The pork chop?"

Justine closed his menu and leaned over to kiss him on the cheek. "Very funny. Cheese fries. That's it. The only acceptable thing to order."

"Got it." He folded his hands on the table. "I do whatever she says," he told me.

"I do too. For twelve years now." I shrugged. "That's the way it has to be with her."

"And I've heard it can get you into trouble." He looked over at Justine and wiggled his eyebrows. "Not too much trouble. Just a little bit."

"Right," I said, smiling at Justine. Emmett was cute, and self-assured, and funny. Based on the three minutes we'd spent together, it was clear he was perfect for Justine. But I had to be sure. "So tell me more about yourself. Hopes and dreams. Aspirations. Favorite subject. Where you see yourself in ten years."

"Whoa!" Emmett jerked his head back. "We haven't even ordered yet."

"We don't have that much time," I reminded him. "You're leaving in two days. Remember?"

The waitress came over, and we ordered the cheese fries and coffees, and Emmett said, "I think I'd like to own a bookstore one day. In a beach town, but I'd keep it open year-round, and it would be, like, a place for people to go when they didn't want to be home but didn't have anywhere else to be."

I nodded and looked over at Justine. She was smiling like a First Lady, all glowy and proud.

"What else can I tell you?" he asked me. And then the waitress brought over the coffees and he said "Thank you" like he meant it, and I just knew he was a good person.

"Have you ever had a pet?" I asked him.

"Um, weird question, Mia, but okay." Justine sipped her coffee. *Sorry she's interviewing you,* she mouthed to Emmett.

"I got this," he replied. "Yup, I have a toy poodle at my mom's place. Murray. He's chill. What about you?"

"I've never had a pet," I said. "But deep down, I think I'm a dog person. So maybe one day."

"We're all dog people," Justine added. "I can just tell, even though I've never had a dog either."

"Do you play sports?" I asked Emmett.

He poured some more milk into his coffee. "Lacrosse."

"That is so typical," I scoffed. "Boston. Lacrosse."

"I know, I know. But I like it." He smiled. "So shoot me some more questions. What else do you want to know about me? I'm an open book."

I sat back. "Will you dance at the prom?"

Justine gasped. "Mia! Stop!"

"What?" My cheeks burned. "I meant, like in general prom, not like our prom. . . ." I knew I should stop talking.

"I always dance," he said. "Sometimes I dance alone."

We looked at him, and we all burst out laughing, and then the cheese fries came.

Emmett stared at them. "We just dig in?" he asked. "I want to make sure I'm doing this right."

"Just dig in." Justine laughed.

We sat there and ate the cheese fries, and I asked him more questions, and everything he said was nice, and genuine, and honest. And it didn't seem like he was putting on a show, or trying to be something he wasn't.

I looked over at him, and then at Justine, and then back at him. And I saw how happy she was—smiling, shoulders relaxed, affectionate with Emmett but not too PDA or anything. Just normal. It all felt calm and peaceful and fun.

And then I realized that if Emmett ever did anything to hurt Justine, I would have to crush him. Seriously. If he ever ripped this happiness away from her, I didn't know what I would do. Something extreme.

I understood why Justine'd had to make Katie, why she'd had to get revenge on Seth.

Feeling hurt yourself was one thing. But watching your friend get hurt, watching someone hurt your friend—no. You couldn't just stand idly by and let that happen with no recourse.

"It was so nice to meet you, Mia," Emmett said when we were in the parking lot.

"Same," I said. "Have a good trip back."

We watched him get into his car, and in my head I said all the things I didn't say aloud: *Be good to her. Don't disappoint her. Don't disappoint me. Please stay as great as I think you are.*

"He's awesome, Justie," I said as she drove me home.

"He is, right?" she asked.

"He really is."

LAST DROPS OF SUMMER

Coconut milk, pineapple, honeydew, spinach

JUSTINE

"So this is it?" I asked Emmett.

We were standing in his driveway. Well, his dad's driveway. It was one of those wraparound ones that were the coolest when you were a kid and you wanted a place to ride your bike. His dad lived in this giant house on the top of a hill in a section of town that I'd never really been to. He had a pool and a tennis court and a mini–movie theater in the basement. His dad took a car service to work in the city every morning. He seemed so scary. I wondered if Emmett lived like this at his mom's house too, but it was a weird question to ask.

"I guess." He shrugged. "I'll try to be here next summer. If my dad's around. Sometimes he's, like, abroad for five months. I don't really get it."

I nodded and swallowed hard.

"We can still see each other, on weekends and stuff." He put his hands on my shoulders. "It's not really that far."

"It's like three hours," I whispered.

"That's nothing," he said. "We'll make it work. I promise."

"Really?"

"Yes."

He moved back a little and kissed me.

"This was my best summer," he said. "And one summer I got to sit front row at the Rolling Stones. So, ya know. I've had some good summers."

"Really?" I asked, even though I knew he was telling the truth.

"Justine, all you've said so far today is *really*. Do you realize that?"

I covered my mouth. "Really?"

He shook his head and kissed me again. "I'm pouring my heart out here, and you're making jokes. That's the Justine way."

"It was my best summer too," I said, finally. "And I mean that. Really."

"I'll dance at the prom. Remember that."

We heard the front door close and saw his dad walking toward us. We pulled apart and tried to make it look casual, like we were just standing out here talking about the weather or something.

"Call me when you get home," I said, chewing the inside of my cheek to keep from crying.

Emmett nodded.

"Promise?"

"Promise."

WELCOME SURPRISES

Watermelon juice, wheatgrass, cucumber, plum

MIA

A million things were so hard to believe.

Justine and I were starting senior year with boyfriends. Okay, mine did go to another school, and no one really knew who he was. But that didn't matter. And Justine's lived in Boston, but it wasn't really *that* far.

We had made two thousand dollars this summer. All on our own.

I'd lost seven pounds.

I knew how to make smoothies. Really good smoothies.

We had humiliated Seth.

I was over him, too.

"So this is the last time I'm going to see you before school starts?" Dennis asked me.

We were sitting cuddled up on the leather couch in his den,

watching some obstacle course competition show on TV, eating sunflower seeds. We weren't really watching the show, but it was on. Background noise.

"I guess so," I said. "It's gonna be weird not seeing you every day."

"I know. And to think I didn't even want to do this job." He shook his head and licked salt off his lips. "It all feels kind of crazy, right?"

"Yeah, but the truth is—I don't think things are ever what we think they're going to be, ya know? It's like what we expect almost never happens."

"Right. I barely even spoke to Justine before this summer."

I laughed a little but tried to hide it. "You don't talk to her much now."

He nodded. "True." Then he looked at me and pulled me up onto his lap. His mom had only gone out to the grocery store to grab some stuff for dinner. She could walk in at any second, but that only made it more exciting.

We stayed like that, cuddled together, kissing on the couch, for a few more minutes, and then we pulled apart a little and looked at each other.

It felt cheesy, to just gaze into each other's eyes like that, but no one else was watching, so the cheesiness didn't matter. And when your boyfriend has gigantic blue ocean eyes like Dennis does, you just want to look at them—look into them—for as long as you possibly can.

SIT BACK AND SMILE

Watermelon juice, lychee, pineapple

JUSTINE

"Do you realize what's happening here?" I asked Mia over the phone.

"What?"

"We're both starting senior year with boyfriends," I said. It was hard to believe. Even though I knew it was true. Even though I said it out loud.

"It's crazy," Mia said. "Really. It feels crazy to me."

"And I know what we're doing with the money," I told her.

"Yeah?" she asked.

"Yeah. I have the perfect plan."

"That's what you always say!" Mia screeched.

"Right. And have I ever steered you wrong?"

She laughed.

I said, "I can't tell you what it is yet. You just have to trust me."

"You always say that, too!"

"Do you want to make sure we're not invisible? Like a fool-proof plan that everyone notices us?" I continued. "On the first day of school."

"Ummm . . ." Mia laughed her nervous laugh.

I sat back in my desk chair. It had been a summer of accomplishments, but we had one more thing to do.

"I'll take that as a yes. We're doing this."

55 NOTICEABLE CHANGE

Pears, strawberries, peaches, fat-free vanilla yogurt

JUSTINE AND MIA

"You're sure?" the guy behind the desk asked us. "I mean, usually this type of thing is for, like, corporate parties, bachelor weekends, marriage proposals. I've never gotten a request like this before."

"We're doing it," we said at the same time.

"All right, more power to ya." He looked up at us after we handed him the money. He typed all our information into the computer.

One of his best, most experienced people, Carl, was on his way in to take us, and we'd be all set.

The whole thing—from start to finish—would take about seven minutes. That was it.

But it would be worth it.

We both got a text.

Alexis: Still wish I was going with you guys, but I get why it's important that I'm here. I'll record everyone's reactions.

We thanked her again and again, but we still felt a little guilty.

"Whatever, she was getting massages in the Catskills all summer" was how we validated it to ourselves. But also, we needed her. We needed her report. We needed her to document it.

Carl arrived. "Ready to go?"

We nodded.

We hopped in and followed all his instructions, and then we were off.

"Right on the football field?" Carl asked us.

"Yup," we said at the same time.

Alexis: Holy crap. You guys. OMG everyone is looking up. Mr. Eckson is muttering to the teachers. I think you need some kind of permit to do this.

Just FYI for next time. LOL. Yeah, right, there will be a next time!

"There's always next summer's earnings." We high-fived.

Alexis: The whole school is outside right now. Literally every person in the school.

We high-fived again.

"I'll admit—I've never done this kind of thing before," Carl said as we got closer.

"Neither have we."

It got noisy then, really noisy, and it was hard to see what was happening, exactly. We felt a loud thump. Kind of a bumpy landing.

So much of life was like that.

And then Carl asked, "You ready?"

We looked at each other then. And smiled.

After all we'd accomplished that summer, we were ready. More than ready.

"Thanks, Carl."

We put our sunglasses on and got out, like it was nothing, like it was something we literally did every day. We held our heads high and walked toward school.

"Who is that?" we heard someone say. We didn't look to see who it was. We didn't care.

"No clue," someone else replied.

We kept walking.

"They took a helicopter to school?" some kid said.

"Is that Mia Remsen and Justine Swirsky?" a girl asked. It sounded like Adia Montgomery, but who knows for sure?

"Mia Remsen and Justine Swirsky took an f'in' helicopter to the first day of school?" another girl squealed. Laurel Peck. We were sure of it.

"They just landed on the football field. Is that allowed? What the—?"

"They are crushing senior year, and it hasn't even started yet," Mike Kim said.

We kept walking.

There was no reason to look anywhere but straight ahead.

We had made it.

ACKNOWLEDGMENTS

First of all, thank you to my extraordinary husband and the love of my life, David Rosenberg, for helping me every single day with ideas for this book, raising our daughters, and offering more encouragement than anyone should ever need. I adore you, and I am beyond grateful for everything.

To my daughters, Aleah and Hazel, you are the shiniest, sparkliest, sunniest parts of my world. I love you more than any words can ever express.

To David and Max, my BBFs (best brothers forever), thank you for everything.

To Alyssa Eisner Henkin, thank you for believing in this book way back in 2007, when I simply wanted to call it *Stalkers*.

To Caroline Abbey, thank you for making this book better than I could have ever imagined. You pushed me to work harder, to stop repeating myself, and to think of these characters in a more thoughtful, careful way. To Elizabeth Tardiff, thanks for the fabulous jacket. Barbara Perris and Barbara Bakowski, your copyediting skills are terrific.

To Mom and Dad, thanks for giving me life and an AOL account.

Bubbie, Zeyda, and Aunt Emily, thanks for all the love, enthusiasm, and support.

To the Rosenbergs, thanks for always asking about the books and helping to promote them.

Many thanks to Rhonda, Melanie, Maddy, Kathleen, Rich, Alex, and the whole BWL community—my home away from home for the past eleven years.

Finally, thank you to my girls (you know who you are) who helped inspire this book. The memories of sitting on America Online back in the day, waiting for people to sign on, make me smile . . . and also cringe. I wouldn't be who I am without your friendship. I am so lucky to have all of you in my life.